I SHOULD
HAVE STAYED
HOME

HORACE McCOY'S

I SHOULD HAVE STAYED HOME

MIDNIGHT
CLASSICS

LONDON / NEW YORK

Library of Congress Catalog Card Number: 95-71065

A catalogue record for this book can be obtained from
the British Library on request

First published in 1938 by Knopf, New York
First published in Great Britain in 1938 by Barker

This edition first published in 1996 by
Serpent's Tail, 4 Blackstock Mews, London N4, and
180 Varick Street, 10th floor, New York, NY 10014

Cover design by Rex Ray

Typeset by CentraCet Limited, Cambridge
Printed in Great Britain by Cox & Wyman Ltd, Reading, Berks.

*...part
one*

...chapter
one

Sitting, sitting, sitting: I had been sitting since I came back from the courtroom, alone and friendless and frightened in the most terrifying town in the world. Looking out the window at that raggledy palm tree in the middle of the bungalow court, thinking Mona, Mona, Mona, wondering what I was going to do without her, that and nothing more: What am I going to do without you? and all of a sudden it was night (there was no purple or pink or mauve), deep, dark night, and I got up and went out to walk, going nowhere in particular, just to walk, to get out of the house where I had lived with Mona and where her smell was still everywhere. I had been wanting to get out for hours, but the sun had kept me in. I was afraid of the sun, not because it was hot but because of what it might do to me in my mind. Feeling the way I did, alone and friendless, with the future very black, I did not want to get out on the streets and see what the sun had to show me, a cheap town filled with cheap stores and cheap people, like the town I had left, identically like any one of ten thousand other small towns in the country – not my Hollywood, not the Hollywood you read about. This is what I was afraid of now, I did not want to take a chance on seeing anything that might have made me wish I had stayed home, and this is why I waited for the darkness, for the night-time. That is when Hollywood is really glamorous and mysterious and you are glad you are here, where miracles are happening all around you, where today you are broke and unknown and tomorrow you are rich and famous. . . .

On Vine Street I went north towards Hollywood Boulevard, crossing Sunset, passing the drive-in stand where the old Paramount lot used to be, seeing young girls and boys in uniform hopping cars, and seeing too, in my mind, the ironic smiles on the faces of Wallace Reid and Valentino and all the other old-time stars who used to work on this very spot, and who now looked down, pitying these girls and boys for working at jobs in Hollywood they might just as well be working at in Waxahachie or Evanston or Albany; thinking if they were going to do this, there was no point in their coming out here in the first place.

The Brown Derby, the sign said, and I crossed the street, not wanting to pass directly in front, hating the place and all the celebrities in it (only because they were celebrities, something I was not), hating the people standing in front, waiting with autograph books, thinking: You'll be fighting for my autograph one of these days, missing Mona terribly now, more than I had all afternoon, because passing this place that was full of stars made me more than ever want to be a star myself and made me more than ever aware of how impossible this was alone, without her help.

I am alone because of Dorothy, I thought. This is all the fault of that shoplifter. This is all Dorothy's fault. I should have grabbed Mona when she jumped up in the courtroom.

6

I should have known from the look on her face what was going to happen.

Mona and I had gone down to the court to let Dorothy have moral support. She had come out to Hollywood to crash the movies too, but she had crashed a department store instead and had systematically stolen a lot of stuff. We knew she wouldn't get off absolutely free, but we thought the judge wouldn't give her more than ninety days, six months at the outside. But the judge sentenced her to the women's prison at Tehachapi for three years and no sooner were the words out of his mouth than Mona was on her feet yelling that he was a fine son of a bitch to be sitting up there dishing out justice and why didn't he hang her and be done with it? I was so astonished I couldn't do anything but sit there with my mouth open. The judge had Mona brought before him, telling her he was going to sentence her to jail for thirty days if she didn't apologize. What she told him to take for himself caused him to give her sixty days instead of thirty.

Later, when court was over, I went to the judge and begged him to let Mona go, but I didn't have any luck.

This is why I was alone. It was all Dorothy's fault; if I had known this was going to happen, I never would have let Mona go down there. All Dorothy's fault, I thought, cursing her in my mind with all the dirty words I could think of, all the filthy ones I could remember the kids in my old gang used to yell at white women as they passed through the neighborhood on their way to work in the nigger whore houses, these are what you are, Dorothy, turning off Vine on to the boulevard, feeling awful and alone, even worse

7

than that time my dog was killed by the Dixie Flyer, but
telling myself in a very faint voice that even like this I was
better off than the fellows I grew up with back in Georgia
who were married and had kids and regular jobs and regular
salaries and were doing the same old thing in the same old
way and would go on doing it forever. They would never
have any fun or adventure, fame would never come to them;
they were like plants in a desert that lived a little while and
then died and became dust and it was as if they had never
lived at all. 'Even like this,' I said to myself, 'I am better off
than they are.' It made me feel good without in any way
relieving the sadness and loneliness I also felt.

Cooper and Gable and lots of others went through what I
am going through, I thought, and if they did it, so can I.
One of these days . . .

Ahead of me, on top the Newberry store, a big neon sign
flashed on and off. It was an outline map of the United
States and these words kept appearing: 'ALL ROADS LEAD TO
HOLLYWOOD – And the Pause that Refreshes. ALL ROADS
LEAD TO HOLLYWOOD – And the Pause that Refreshes. ALL
ROADS LEAD TO HOLLYWOOD –'

...*chapter two*

I do not remember what time I got back to the bungalow. It was late, sometime after midnight. All the side streets were deserted and the little houses were quiet and still and dark. There was very little hell raised in this neighborhood; this part of Hollywood was like the residential section of any small town after midnight. This was where you lived when you first started in pictures and from this point you gradually worked westward to Beverly Hills, the Promised Land.

A man was sitting on the steps of the bungalow waiting for me. There was not much light in the court and all I could see was that it was a man. He stood up as I approached.

'Good evening,' he said.

I thought he must be mixed up in his bungalows.

'I've had a hard time finding you,' he said, turning towards me. Then I recognized him, trembling all over again. He was the judge who had sentenced Dorothy and Mona, Judge Boggess.

'Oh, good evening, sir,' I said, not saying anything else, wondering how he had found me and what he wanted.

'Can't we go inside?' he asked finally.

I led the way inside the living-room and turned on the light. He took off his hat, looking around, and sat down on

9

the davenport. He picked up a copy of a newspaper that was lying there, the Oklahoma City *Daily News*, and looked at it.

'Are you from Oklahoma City?'

'No, sir – that's Mona's. She's from a little town near Oklahoma City.'

'Where does she live?'

'Here.'

'Here?'

'Yes, sir.'

'Does the other girl live here too? Dorothy?'

'She lived over there,' I said, pointing out the darkened window to the bungalow across the court, behind that raggledy palm tree.

'Unfortunate about Dorothy – '

'Yes, sir.'

'Well,' he said, putting down the newspaper, looking at me thoughtfully, 'I'll tell you why I'm here. I've been thinking over what you said to me in my chambers this afternoon about Mona. Maybe I was a bit too severe with her – '

'Oh, she should have been punished after that scene she made,' I said. 'You couldn't do anything else with all those people in the courtroom. It'd be a fine thing if anybody could jump up in a courtroom and say anything they pleased. What Mona should have done was to apologize when she had the chance.'

'That's it exactly,' he said, nodding. 'I don't want to keep this girl in jail and interfere with her picture career – and on the other hand I can't let her out until she gives some indication that she's sorry for what she did – and said.'

I could see that all right.

'I think you're perfectly right,' I said. 'Maybe if I went and had a talk with her – '

He shook his head.

'I don't think that'll work. I don't think she'll give in for you or anybody else. How would this be – suppose you wrote me a letter of apology and signed her name, pretending it came from her. I realize that's not exactly ethical, but I want to do this girl a favor and that's the only way. I don't mind being a trifle unethical if that's the only way I can serve justice – and this letter'll put me in the clear. If she's as important to you as you say – '

'She's pretty important, Judge,' I said. 'She's the only friend I've got in town. I'll be glad to write the letter, but what'll I say?'

'You get some paper and a pencil. I'll tell you what to say.'

'Yes, sir. Judge, this is wonderful of you,' I said, going to the desk to get the pencil and paper.

...*chapter three*

It was around three o'clock that same morning when Mona was released. I was waiting in the jailer's office when one of the turnkeys brought her in. Her face was paler than usual.

'Hello, Mona,' I said.

'How'd this happen?' she asked the jailer.

'You got a commutation,' he said. 'The judge cut your sentence to twelve hours.'

'Mighty white of the old son of a bitch,' Mona said.

'Is that any way to talk?' the jailer asked. 'Get that tramp outta here,' he told me.

'Come on, Mona, let's go,' I said, taking her by the arm, afraid she would get into another jam. I led her outside to the street.

'How'd this happen?' she asked.

'What're you asking me for? I don't know.'

'Then what're you doing here? Don't tell me there's a coincidence like that left in the world,' she said sarcastically. 'How'd it happen?'

'I don't know, I tell you. The judge simply let you out, I suppose. Maybe he's not as tough as you thought he was.'

'Don't tell me. That old son of a bitch's heart is as hard as this sidewalk –'

'Well, if you must know, I went out to his house and had a talk with him,' I said finally. I opened the door of her jalopy, helped her in, went round to the other side, and got under the wheel.

'Thanks – ' she said.

We rolled along Broadway towards Sunset.

'Get a letter from home this afternoon?' she asked, pointing to the gasoline gauge, that registered three-fourths full. 'You were broke this morning.'

'Oh, that,' I said. 'Abie – at the market. I borrowed a dollar.'

'You get any calls today?'

'No.'

'Did I?'

'No.'

She looked out the window, in the direction of Olvera Street. I knew what she was thinking.

'After all,' I said, 'there're twenty thousand other extras in this town. Nobody can work all the time.'

'A hell of a life, isn't it?' she said, looking at me, shaking her head slowly.

'I think it's marvelous,' I said. 'One of these days we'll look back on this and say: "They were the good old days." We'll have plenty of material for the fan-magazine writers when we do get to be stars,' I said, turning off Broadway on to Sunset, towards Hollywood. . . .

...*chapter four*

The following morning I was in the kitchen fixing some coffee when Mona came in with a newspaper.

'Seen this?'

'Not yet.'

'Take a look. Right there,' she said, holding the paper so I could see it, pointing to a story on the first page of the second section.

BOGGESS RELEASES FILM PLAYER

WHO WAS SENTENCED FOR CONTEMPT

Mona Matthews, 26-year-old movie extra, who was yesterday sentenced to sixty days in jail for contempt of court by Judge Emil Boggess, was released late last night after serving only twelve hours. She is the girl who created a sensation in the courtroom yesterday when Dorothy Trotter, also a film extra, was sentenced to prison for three years after pleading guilty to grand theft. The Matthews girl yelled curses at Judge Boggess for passing the sentence on her friend.

Miss Matthews was released after she had written an apology to Judge Boggess.

'As far as I'm concerned the case is closed,' Judge

Boggess said. 'I have no desire to keep the girl in jail simply for the sake of punishing her. I realize she spoke in the heat of shock and anger and I didn't want to put her in jail at all, but I had no other course to pursue if I were to uphold the dignity and fairness of our courts.'

Thus Judge Boggess again indicates why his associates call him the Great Humanitarian.

I finished reading and looked at her.

'I thought you went out to his house and had a talk with him. Whose idea was that letter of apology?'

'Now, wait a minute, Mona – '

'He thought up that letter business, didn't he?'

'Now, look – '

'You're goddam right he did. "The Great Humanitarian." Phooey!'

'You've got him all wrong,' I said.

'The hell I have. You don't think he was doing me a favor, do you? He's running for re-election and that story'll get him votes. The morons who read that paper'll believe he's really got a conscience. "The Great Humanitarian."'

'What do you care as long as you're out of jail?' I asked.

'I'd rather have stayed in jail than help that louse get re-elected. Jesus,' she said, looking at me, shaking her head, 'if only I had your trusting nature.'

'Anybody here?' came a shout from the living-room. In a moment a young fellow of about my age came into the kitchen. I had never seen him before.

'Well, for Christ's sake,' he said when he saw Mona. 'Welcome home. How was the hoosegow?'

15

'Sam – ' Mona said, going into his outstretched arms. They hugged without kissing and then stepped back, looking at each other.

'My – you're looking prosperous,' she said, feeling the material of his coat.

'Sure,' Sam said, grinning. 'Remember what I told you a year ago? That one of these days I was going to be the best-dressed man in this town?'

'You're gaining on it,' Mona said. 'You're looking grand.'

'Well, I must say you're looking grand too – considering you've done time,' Sam said, grinning.

Mona looked from me to Sam.

'This is Ralph Carston,' she said. 'Sam Lally.'

We shook hands. Instinctively I disliked him. This is what comes of always leaving the front door open, I thought.

'Hello, Ralph,' he said, very friendly. 'I used to do that – '

'What?'

'What you're doing. I used to be Mona's chief cook and bottlewasher. Does he sleep on the davenport too?' he asked Mona.

She nodded, looking at me sidewise.

'It's marvelous the way she collected guys who are down and out,' Sam said to me. 'She's always – '

'Let's go in the other room,' she said, taking him by the arm, leading him off.

I went on making the coffee until I heard the kitchen door close and then I realized that Mona felt guilty about something or she never would have done this. The hell with them,

I thought, turning off the burner under the coffee pot, going out the back door to the market round the corner. . . .

When I got back, Lally was gone and Mona was in the kitchen.

'You mustn't pay any attention to Sam,' she said.

'What do you mean?' I asked. 'I didn't pay any attention to him. I don't pay any attention to people I don't like.'

'Now, cut that out. I knew you were burned. I could tell by the expression on your face – '

'Well, after all, there's nothing like meeting the guy who used to sleep in your bed,' I said. 'How long ago was that?'

'Six months. There was nothing between us. No more than there is between you and me. I simply gave him a lift.'

'He certainly seems to be doing all right now. That suit he had on must've cost a hundred bucks.'

'A hundred and fifty. You know what he's doing?'

'I remember the name from somewhere,' I said, 'but I wasn't sufficiently interested to worry about it.'

'Mrs. Smithers,' she said. 'You've heard of Mrs. Smithers.'

I had heard of Mrs. Smithers, all right. Her name was in the movie column every day. Her husband had died and left her a lot of money and she had come to Hollywood and taken charge of the social register.

'Yes,' I said.

'That's what Sam does. He's living with her. That's where he got all those clothes.'

I remembered now. Sam Lally. You never saw her name in the paper without his.

'I didn't know he was living with her.'

'Sure, she wouldn't have it any other way. She'll wear him out in another six months. She's a nymphomaniac, you know.'

'A what?'

'A nymphomaniac. She can't get enough.'

I took the toast out of the oven.

'You'll meet her tonight.'

'I'll meet her? How?'

'We're going to her party. She's invited us. That's why Sam came here. She wants to meet the girl who called Judge Boggess a son of a bitch.'

'She doesn't want to meet me,' I said. 'I didn't call Judge Boggess a son of a bitch.'

Mona laughed.

'I know you didn't, but I explained to Sam that I wouldn't come without you. He phoned her and she said she'd be delighted for you to come too.'

'But,' I said, thinking of Lally's hundred-and-fifty-dollar suit, 'I haven't got any clothes.'

'Wear your blue suit. This is your chance to get a close-up of a real Hollywood party. I wouldn't miss it for the world.'

'Say, there'll be plenty of time for parties after we're stars,' I said.

'Everybody who's anybody in Hollywood'll be there – producers, directors, stars – and you never can tell when one of them might be interested in you. You don't think I want to go just because it's a party, do you?'

'I don't know –'

'Well, I don't. Nobody goes to these things just because

they're parties, not like they do back where we come from, to have a good time. People go to Hollywood parties because there's always a chance to help themselves. This might be the break we're both waiting for.'

'I still don't want to go,' I said. 'You know how I feel about meeting important people. You know how I hate the Brown Derby and places like that.'

...*chapter five*

Mrs. Smithers lived in Beverly Hills on one of those wide, curving streets, in a house that was almost hidden by palm trees. The street in front of her house was lined on both sides with automobiles. We had to park two blocks away.

'I'll disgrace you sure as hell,' I said to Mona as we approached the house. 'I haven't the faintest idea what to do or say at one of these things.'

'Don't be self-conscious now,' she said. 'Just remember that practically everybody who'll be here was once in the same fix as we are.'

The first person we saw when we got inside was Sam Lally. He had on a tuxedo that fitted him like a glove. He came over to us, grinning, and shook hands. I felt more nervous than ever and I began to get sore. There was a big crowd in the living-room and most of the men had on tuxedos.

'Well, well, well – ' Lally said. 'Hello, hello, hello – I'm glad to see you.'

You'd think this bastard owned the place instead of being just a gigolo, I thought. – 'Hello,' I said.

'Ethel,' Lally called, and a big woman dressed in purple velvet came over. 'Mrs. Smithers, may I present Mona

Matthews and – ' he looked at me, trying to remember my name.

You bastard, I thought. – 'Carston,' I told him. 'Ralph Carston.'

'I'm so glad to see you, my dear,' Mrs. Smithers said, taking Mona's hand and holding it. 'And you too – Ralph,' she said to me. With her other hand she took my arm and held it, looking from Mona to me, smiling. 'You don't think it's odd that I sent Sammy to invite you to my party?'

'Of course not, Mrs. Smithers,' Mona said. 'We were very much flattered.'

'As a matter of fact,' Mrs. Smithers said, 'Sam has spoken to me often about you. You're a very kind person.'

She looked at me again, and I thought I knew what she was thinking – that Mona was doing the same thing for me she had once done for Sam. Well, I thought, looking at her, at least she's not buying my clothes like you are his.

'Come, dear,' Mrs. Smithers said, leading us to the living-room. This room was lower than the hall, four steps down. She stopped at the head of the steps, clapping her hands together.

'Everybody!' she said. 'Everybody!'

In a moment the people were quiet, looking at her.

'I want all you famous people to meet a real celebrity. This is Mona Matthews – and Ralph Carston, her escort. Mona is the girl, you will remember, who got the headlines yesterday by calling one of our most distinguished judges a dirty name right out loud in open court where everybody would hear her. For which, I might add, she did a few hours in jail for contempt – '

21

'Hello Mona,' somebody shouted from the back of the room near the piano. 'I'm an ex-convict myself.'

'We're all birds of a feather,' somebody else said.

A woman sitting at the piano started playing *The Prisoner's Song* and in a moment everybody was joining in the words.

'Now, go right ahead, my dear, and have a good time,' Mrs. Smithers said, moving away towards the front door. The people in the living-room started making up words about Mona to the tune of *The Prisoner's Song* and I looked at her, feeling a little better now that I realized most of them were drunk and therefore wouldn't pay so much attention to my clothes. Mona was smiling.

'This is a big moment in my life,' she whispered to me.

'But most of them are drunk,' I said.

'They're still celebrities,' she answered.

Three or four girls came over, laughing, and took Mona by the arm, leading her down into the living-room. I stood there for a moment and then went back towards the front door because I didn't know what else to do. There were some more people coming in. I recognized Grace Briscoe, the big star, shaking hands with Mrs. Smithers and Sam. As she came into the entrance hall she stopped at a table where a man sat and handed him a ten-dollar bill. He thanked her and put it in a tin box.

It's a funny party where they invite you and then charge you, I thought. They didn't charge us.

'Where's your drink?' Lally asked, coming over to me.

'I haven't got one,' I said.

'Sam,' Mrs. Smithers said, 'get Ralph a drink. We'll be out on the patio'

She led me out into the patio, where the swimming-pool was. It was a big tile pool and had blue and amber lights under the water. Several people were swimming.

'This is lovely,' I said.

'Like it?'

'I certainly do. I think you were nice to ask me. I didn't want to come'

'You're not sorry, I hope.'

'No, ma'am.'

'Wouldn't you like to go swimming?'

I shook my head.

'No, ma'am, thanks. I haven't got a swimming suit.'

'That doesn't matter. Look,' she said, laughing, pointing to the people in the pool. One of them, a girl, was on the bank. She was completely nude. 'You mustn't let a little thing like a swimming suit keep you from going swimming.'

Lally came out with the drink just then.

'Sam,' she said, 'this is charming. This is the most charming thing I've seen in years.'

'What?' Lally asked.

'Your friend here. He's blushing.'

Lally looked at me and then around at the nude girl who was still on the bank, and then back at me. He laughed too.

'This is Hollywood, old man,' he said, 'where morality never crosses the city limits.'

'Jesus,' I said to myself, thinking this was wonderful; not the naked girl, but to be in a town where nobody paid any attention to what anybody else did. In the town I was brought up in, what everybody did was everybody else's business and somebody was always trying to tell you how to live your life.

'I think he's shocked,' Lally said, laughing again. 'He's still blushing.'

'I'm not blushing,' I answered.

'If this makes you blush, wait'll you get acquainted,' Mrs Smithers said.

I did not say anything, taking a swallow of the drink. It was the first liquor I had ever tasted in my life.

When I came downstairs from the dressing-rooms beside the pool, I had on a pair of wet trunks I had borrowed from a man who had just come out. There was nobody in the pool but the same girl, but there were several people sitting in the patio talking. When the naked girl saw I had on trunks, she pointed her finger at me and began jeering.

'Hoohoohoohoo,' she said. 'A sissy, a sissy!'

She was standing in the shallow part of the pool with only her head and shoulders out of the water, but the lights along the side, under the water, made it transparent, and you could see everything she had, even the place where the Indian shot her. I dived in the deep end and swam around a minute or two to get used to the water. She swam over to me.

'Hello,' she said.

'Hello,' I said.

'Do I know you?'

'I don't think so,' I said. 'I'm new here.'

'Good,' she said. 'I like people I don't know because if I don't know them I don't dislike them. I'm Fay Capeheart.'

'I'm Ralph Carston.'

'You in pictures?'

'No.'

'Well, you're smart. I am.'

'I know. I've seen you.'

'What do you do?'

'I'm just trying to be in pictures. I'm just an extra – when I can get it.'

'My God!' she exclaimed. 'What desecration! How ever did you get in here?'

I told her how I had happened to come.

'I don't know anybody but the girl who brought me. That's why I came swimming.'

'You're better off not knowing anybody here too,' she said. 'They're all phoney.'

'What are you doing here, then?' I asked.

'Publicity,' she said. 'I do a lot of things I don't want to do because I'm in the movies and personal publicity is pretty important. Smithers gives the biggest parties in town and therefore she gets the most space. Coming to her parties is like buying an ad in one of the trade papers. My friend, you don't know how well off you are – being an extra.'

'Oh, I don't know,' I said.

'Take my word for it – you are.'

A couple of men walked by the pool where we were. One of them, the big one, was dressed in slacks and a sweatshirt, and the other one, the little one, had on a linen suit. They were talking in loud voices and each one had a drink in his hand.

'All this stuff about a united front is just so much crap,' the little one said.

'How you talk!' said the other one.

They sat down in a couple of deck chairs, not paying any attention to us.

Fay leaned over to me and whispered:

'A couple of high-powered writers. This'll be good.'

'Certainly it is,' the little one said. 'You guys act like a lot of college freshmen. Every goddam one of you is sore at me because I resigned from the Guild. You've got a lot of guts talking to me about unity. I've got scars on both shoulder-blades from carrying banners in the Sacco-Vanzetti case long before you social climbers took it up, and in thousands of other picket lines, too. Didn't Bob Minor and I get out of Alabama a jump ahead of the mob that wanted to lynch us for going to bat for the Scottsboro boys? You're a lot of goddam parlor Communists. You guys get new fads every year.'

'How you talk!' the other one said.

'Yeah, how I talk!' the little one replied. 'Where the hell were all you united-front guys when the Federated Crafts were out on strike? I didn't see any one of you in the picket line around the theaters. You were afraid to jeopardize that two grand a week you're getting.'

'How you talk! Aren't we sending bandages and medical supplies to the Loyalists? Aren't we supporting the Anti-Nazi League?'

26

'Huckleberries,' the little one said. 'You support the Anti-Nazi League because every producer in this lousy town's a Jew and you think he thinks you're being heroic because you're a gentile fighting his fight. Don't tell me. If all the producers were Nazis you guys couldn't wait to start a pogrom. Good God, fellow, be honest.'

Fay looked at me, shaking her head feebly.

'Why don't you two stop arguing and fight?' she asked them.

The two writers looked at her, seeing her for the first time.

'Whoops – a mermaid,' the big one said, throwing his drink into a flowerbed and diving into the pool with all his clothes on. Fay swam quickly to the other side and climbed out, running upstairs to the dressing-room.

The writer came up, puffing and blowing, and I swam over, pushing him into the shallow part of the pool where he could stand up. The other writer, the little one, was still sitting in his chair, drinking as if nothing had happened.

'Nice going, Heinrich,' he said quietly.

I helped him to the bank and he got out, walking away, not even saying thank you. There was a lot of noise from the house now, people laughing and talking and singing; but I went on swimming around, alone now, swimming on my back, looking at the stars, thinking these were the same stars that were shining on my home town, where everybody was asleep now, where everybody would get up tomorrow and start doing the same old thing all over again, asking myself if it could really be true that I was swimming in a pool in Beverly Hills at a house where all the movie stars were:

27

imagining I was a movie star myself, feeling that I had been here a long time, even before I was born, in the days when De Mille and Lasky and the others were just starting the business. . . .

I looked around and Mrs. Smithers was watching me.

'You've been in there an hour. Don't you think that's long enough?'

'I didn't know I'd been in so long,' I said, paddling over to the side. 'This is wonderful.'

'You've been in long enough for at least a dozen people to ask me who the Greek god in the pool is. Are you waiting for some attractive woman to come in without her clothes?'

'Oh, no, ma'am,' I said, climbing out.

'I thought maybe you were waiting for me to come in,' she said.

'Oh, no, ma'am.'

'You're charming – utterly charming,' she said, smiling, looking at me. 'And what a beautiful body you've got!'

'Thank you, ma'am.'

'Are you an athlete?'

'No, ma'am. I used to play football in high school, that's all.'

'You like to swim, though.'

'Yes, ma'am'

'Well, you come swimming here any time you want to. Any time at all.'

'Thank you, ma'am.'

'I want you to join the party. Now run along and put your clothes on – but it does seem such a sacrilege – '

I walked off, not knowing exactly what she meant, but

having a funny feeling at the base of my spine, the same kind of feeling I remembered having when I was about thirteen years old when I would go on picnics with the Bible class and Mrs. Smith, the teacher, would get me alone in the woods and sit opposite me, telling me about Christ and all the apostles, but all the time opening her legs, letting me see the tops of her black stockings and her underwear, pretending not to notice that I was looking. . . .

When I put my clothes on and came downstairs into the patio, Mona was sitting on a wicker davenport with some girl.

'You really gave that pool a black eye, didn't you?' Mona said. 'Here, I want you to meet somebody. Miss Eubanks, this is Ralph Carston.'

'How do you do?' she said. 'Excuse me,' she said, standing up, walking away.

'Wasn't that Laura Eubanks?' I asked.

'That was Laura Eubanks, all right – the one and only.'

'She acted like she was sore. Did I interrupt something?'

'I'll say you did. Well – live and learn. I guess you just can't tell any more about anybody.' She looked at me. 'We're doing all right, aren't we?'

'I'll say.'

'Yes, sir. Eubanks on the make for me, and Smithers on the make for you. We'll be moving out of that little bungalow court any day now.'

'She wasn't on the make for me,' I said.

'You may not have recognized it, but that's what it was. As innocent as you are, a woman would have to start taking your pants off before you got suspicious.'

29

My flesh began to crawl a little.

'You better lay off the liquor,' I said.

'I guess I had,' she answered, nodding.

Somebody started singing, a man, in the living-room behind us, in a deep, rich voice. I turned around and looked.

'Hey,' I whispered to Mona. 'Look over there in that corner by the living-room door.'

She turned around and looked.

'I don't see anything,' she said. 'What is it?'

'That man and woman in each other's arms.'

She looked again, and in a moment she spoke to me over her shoulder, still looking.

'What about it?'

'Why, he's a nigger,' I said.

She turned around to me quickly.

'You mustn't use that word,' she said. 'There's no niggers out here. It's colored men. He's a colored man.'

'Indians are colored, too,' I said, still looking at them. 'The point is she's a white woman. Why, the – '

'Now, wait a minute,' she said, laying her hand on my arm. I could feel the muscles jumping against her hand. 'You stop being a professional Southerner. You mind your own business – '

'This is my business,' I said, starting to get up. She jumped to her feet and shoved me down in the chair, standing over me, leaning her head in close.

'You goddam fool – listen to me,' she said in a tense voice, putting her hands on the arm of the chair, hemming me in; 'if she doesn't mind, you shouldn't. You make a scene here

30

and you may as well pack up and move on. You want to be in pictures, don't you?'

'Certainly, I do.'

'Well, then, mind your own business. Everybody in Hollywood is here. Start a ruckus and you'll be ruined before you even get inside a studio. You'll have to put up with a lot worse than this – and it just so happens that the cheap feels they're getting now is the nicest part of their affair. They've been sleeping together for months. That's Helga Carruthers.'

'I'm sorry,' I said.

'You ought to be. Don't you know this is one town where nobody pays any attention to what anybody else does?'

This surprised me. This is exactly what I had thought a little while ago, only I was thinking about Fay Capeheart swimming in the nude. Mona's right, I thought. Then I realized the reason I thought it was wonderful that nobody paid any attention to the naked girl in swimming was because the sight of her in the water with no clothes on had pleased me very much. This other, this black man and Helga Carruthers, I hadn't thought so wonderful because it displeased me very much. That was why I wanted to do something about it. 'I've got to get over that,' I told myself. 'That's the way all reformers are; they let alone the things that please them and fight the things that don't. I mustn't be like that.'

'You cool off,' Mona said.

'I'm cooled,' I said. 'I don't give a damn what that dinge does. He can lay her at Hollywood and Vine for all I care.'

She straightened up, folding her arms.

'That's better,' she said. 'I'm going to teach you tolerance if I have to kill you.'

I looked around again. A couple of people were coming out a door near Helga Carruthers and she and her black lover quickly stopped kissing each other, pretending to be very formal. I thought about her pictures on the covers of all the movie magazines and the stories they carried about her home life.

Jesus, I thought, if they only knew . . .

The man with the deep, rich voice stopped singing and there was a little applause. Then somebody yelled: 'Come and get it, come and get it,' and there was a hubbub inside.

'We may as well eat,' Mona said.

'Do we have food too?' I asked.

'What do you think they charged everybody ten bucks to get in for? You get all the food you can eat and all the liquor you can drink.'

'We didn't pay ten bucks.'

'Smithers paid it for us. This is a benefit.'

'A benefit? For who?'

'For the Scottsboro boys. You know who the Scottsboro boys are?'

'No.'

'Remind me to tell you,' she said, leading the way into the dining-room.

...*chapter six*

There were stories in the two morning papers about Mrs. Smithers' party for the Scottsboro boys, but neither Mona's name nor mine was mentioned in the list of guests. I felt so disappointed I could have cried. All night I had thought about what the folks back home would say when they got those clippings with my name mentioned along with all the big stars, how they would think I was doing so well. I wrote the letter anyway.

Mona was still asleep upstairs, so I fixed myself some toast and coffee and walked over to the Excelsior studios to try and see Mr. Balter, the man who brought me out to Hollywood. The cop at the information desk telephoned his office and said he wasn't in yet.

'May I wait?' I asked him.

'Help yourself,' he said.

I had been trying to see Mr. Balter off and on for two or three months to find out what had happened to my test. I had decided a long time ago that the test couldn't have been any good, else the studio would have telephoned me before. But I thought the least Mr. Balter could do would be to see me and explain what was wrong. I felt I was entitled to that much. I didn't ask him to bring me to Hollywood, he asked me to come. That was six months ago when I was playing Joe in *They Knew What They Wanted* in the Little Theater back home. Mr. Balter was in the audience one night, and after the performance our director brought him back and introduced him as a talent scout from Hollywood. Mr. Balter said he thought my performance was fine and asked me if I'd be interested in going into the movies, and that if I would the Excelsior studios would pay my expenses to have a test made.

That was why I came out. About a month later they made the test and that was the last I had heard from them. I tried and tried to get Mr. Balter on the telephone, but his secretary wouldn't let me talk to him. She kept taking my name and number and saying she would have him call me, but, of course, he didn't. I should have known from this that it was hopeless, but I knew if I kept coming to the studio and waiting that one of these days I would see him going through the reception room – and if I ever saw him face to face, he was going to have a hard time telling me he would call me later.

I went to the cop again and asked him to see if Mr. Balter had come in yet. He shoved back the telephone and looked at me, frowning.

'Son,' he said, 'this is the fourth time I've called him in an hour. I'll call him all day if you want me to. That's my job. But it's pretty plain to me that he doesn't want to see you.'

'It's plain to me too,' I said.

'Well, I'm not supposed to give lectures, but I hate to see

a nice kid like you bumping your head against a brick wall. You've been coming over here three months now and you haven't got to first base. Why don't you forget it and go back to Mississippi?'

'Georgia,' I said.

A woman came up with a little girl four or five years old, interrupting him.

'I'm Mrs. Sisbee. I have an appointment with Mr. Midwig.'

He dialled a number and got an okay, writing out a pass.

I wish it was that easy for me, I thought.

'Through that door, down the hall, last office on the right,' he said, pressing the button that controlled the electric lock. As Mrs. Sisbee started through the door, she bent down and smoothed the little girl's hair.

'Shirley Temple started all that,' he said. 'That woman's sure her kid is better than Shirley Temple.'

'Maybe she is,' I said. 'How can you tell until she has a chance?'

He looked at me, smiling.

'It's all mathematical, son,' he said. 'It's like filling an inside straight. Just enough people do it to keep everybody else trying.'

'Won't you try Mr. Balter again?' I asked.

When I got back to the court, I heard the phone ringing in our bungalow, and when it kept on ringing I started running, thinking it might be a call from Central Casting or maybe Mr. Balter. Every time it rung I thought that. I ran in and grabbed it.

35

It was a woman named Hollingsworth, a fan-magazine writer, who said she wanted to interview Mona. I asked her to hold the phone a minute.

'Mona, Mona,' I called. 'Mona – '

There was no answer.

'She isn't here, but she'll be back in a minute, I know. Can you call back?'

'Do you think it'll be all right if I come over and wait for her?'

'I suppose so.'

'Where do you live?'

I gave her the address on Vine Street and hung up, wondering less about why a fan-magazine writer wanted to interview Mona than I did about where she was and why she had gone out leaving the telephone with nobody to answer it. That was the first lesson I had learned in Hollywood, that is the one thing an extra does not do – leave the telephone unguarded, not for a single moment. That was the very time Central Casting always called, and when there was no answer they called somebody else. Some extras, the old-timers, had long extension cords on their telephones and even took them into the johnny with them. They tell a lot of funny stories about that. . . .

I heard a noise at the front door and turned and there was Mrs. Smithers.

'Good morning, good morning,' she said. 'May I come in?'

'Yes, ma'am,' I said, surprised. 'Come in.'

She came in, looking around the room.

'So this is where you live,' she said.

'Yes, ma'am. Won't you sit down?'

'Yes, I will – for a few minutes. Sammy went on a couple of errands for me and is coming back to get me. Where is – er – what's her name?'

'Mona? I don't know. She's around somewhere.'

'Well, well,' Mrs. Smithers said, sitting down. 'Tell me, did you have a good time last night?'

'Yes, ma'am. I had a wonderful time. It was the first time I'd ever seen anything like that.'

'You mustn't let it be the last. Would you like to go swimming this afternoon?'

'I don't think I'd better,' I said. 'I'd like to, all right, but I better stick by the phone.'

She kept looking at me the way she did last night in the swimming-pool, that gave me that funny feeling at the base of my spine, but it didn't bother me any more because now I knew what it was.

'Not with you,' I thought. 'You're too old.'

'Come – sit here beside me,' she said, patting the davenport with her hand; and I went over and sat down, not wanting to offend her. She smiled at me. 'You dear, unspoiled boy,' she said. 'You dear, dear boy. I know we're going to be such good friends. I'm going to help you a lot.'

She placed her hand on my leg and I started trembling, not from the touch of her hand or anything like that; I was thinking if Mona should come in now and catch us here like this, I'd have a difficult time explaining that I was just being polite.

'Why are you frowning so?' she asked, leaning over close to me. She had on make-up an inch thick.

'I was thinking – '

'About what?'

'Oh, about last night. How wonderful it was.'

'Silly – that's nothing to frown about.'

'I was frowning because I was thinking maybe I wouldn't get to go to another party like that.'

'Ah!' she said, taking out a cigarette and lighting it. 'There'll be loads of parties like that. The first thing you know, you'll be having them yourself. You'll be the host – I'll bet that within a year's time you'll be one of the biggest stars in pictures.'

'Do you really think so?' I asked.

'You will if I have anything to do with it,' she said. 'And I think I will. Most of the people in this town who can help you are my friends.'

I knew that was true. 'Maybe you aren't too old, at that,' I thought.

The back door slammed and we both jumped up as if we'd been shot. It was Mona, with a shopping-bag full of groceries. She saw us from the kitchen, put the bag on the table, and came in and stood looking at us, not saying anything for a moment.

'Good morning,' Mrs. Smithers said.

'Morning,' Mona said. 'Fun, hunh?'

'Mrs. Smithers just dropped in to say hello,' I said.

'That was sweet of her.' Mona looked at Mrs. Smithers. 'You seem to have survived very well.'

'God knows, I've given enough of them.'

Nobody said anything for a moment. Mona was looking at Mrs. Smithers, who was fidgeting nervously with her cigarette. From Mona's attitude and tone I knew there was danger ahead, and Mrs. Smithers knew it too. I wanted to say something, but I didn't know what. I didn't want to offend either one of them. Mrs. Smithers put her cigarette in an ash-tray and finally stood up.

'Well – ' she said.

Mona still didn't say anything.

'Don't go,' I said to Mrs. Smithers. 'I thought you were going to wait for Lally.'

'Perhaps,' she said, glancing at Mona, 'I'd better wait outside.'

'That's silly,' I said. 'You wait right here.'

'Well – '

'Of course you will. Please sit down.'

'Let her wait outside if she wants to,' Mona said.

There it was. This was what I was trying to avert. Mrs. Smithers pressed her lips together, pressing the blood out of them.

'Mona!' I said.

'Oh, it doesn't bother me. I was thinking of you. It'd be much better for you if she waited outside. You see,' she said slowly. 'I think I know what she's after.'

Mrs. Smithers let her lips go, opening them in a faint smile.

'You don't mean that, my dear,' she said in a level tone.

'Who the hell do you think you are kidding? What other interest could you possibly have in us?'

'Mona!' I said again.

She laughed, looking at Mrs. Smithers.

'Look,' she said. 'I appreciate your asking me to the party last night – even if I do know what prompted the invitation. But I don't think that gives you the license to try to suck this kid into an intrigue with you. Aren't there enough men in Hollywood for you without picking on him?'

'I'll walk outside with you,' I said to Mrs. Smithers.

She smiled at me, patting her arm, and suddenly, in that moment, I felt very sorry for her.

'Mona,' I said, 'Mrs. Smithers came to see me. If you don't like it, suppose you take a walk. I guess I've got a right to have my friends visit me.'

'What right?' she said, baring her teeth a little.

'Why are you so upset?' Mrs. Smithers asked. 'I only want to help him – help both of you.'

'We don't need your help.'

'I have no designs on either one of you. I'm not going to take him away from you. I know how much he means to you.'

'He doesn't mean a goddam thing.'

'Not now, my dear – you aren't fooling me either. I know more about you than you think I do. You're the type that must have someone to mother.'

Mona stood glaring at her. I thought it was time for me to say something. I took Mrs. Smithers by the arm.

'We'll wait outside.'

Mrs. Smithers hesitated for a moment and then went out with me into the court, walking towards the street.

'I'm awfully sorry,' I said.

'Forget it,' she answered. 'I understand. She's a pathological case. She's badly frustrated. You know what she should do? She should go back home. She's got no business in Hollywood.'

'I guess there're a lot of us like that,' I said.

'Not you, dear boy – not you. You've got a future. Do you mind if I have a hand in your future?'

'I should say not.'

She opened her purse, took out a hundred-dollar bill, and offered it to me.

'Oh, I can't take that,' I said.

She smiled, putting the bill in my coat pocket.

'I'll never miss it – and you'll need some clothes.'

We came out on Vine Street and stood on the curbing. The sun was shining brightly, the kind of a sun I hated for what it did to the town, and then I was a little surprised to discover that it was softer than usual and not so glaring, that it was more golden. I felt the hundred-dollar bill in my pocket, wadded up into a little ball, and then, for the first time since I had been in Hollywood, I was not afraid of the sun. All at once I began to look at all the automobiles that passed and the people in them, not ashamed any more, not frightened, daring to look everybody in the face, not hating the celebrities, because I knew that soon I was going to be one myself. I knew too that as far as Mrs. Smithers was concerned I was completely sunk. Now she had bought me – but since last night I had changed completely inside. Now I realized that nobody can beat the movie game without help – and the quicker you play ball, the quicker you succeed. The people at Mrs. Smithers's party had the right idea. You had to kiss you-know-whats.

'Also,' Mrs. Smithers was saying, 'you'll need an agent.'

'I'm only an extra,' I said. 'I can't get an agent. I've tried. I sit for hours in their offices and they won't see me.'

'All you need is influence. I want you to go see Stanley Bergerman. Can you remember that name?'

'Sure, Bergerman. I've heard of him.'

'I think he's the best agent in town. I'll phone him you're coming out. He'll see you.'

'Thank you, ma'am. I'll take my scrapbook out with me – '

She seemed surprised that I had a scrapbook.

'Have you ever done any acting?'

'Oh, yes, ma'am. In the Little Theater back home. That's how I came out here in the first place. A talent scout from Excelsior brought me out for a test – but nothing ever came of it.'

'That's fine,' she said.

A big car rolled up beside us, driven by a chauffeur in brown livery, and stopped. Lally got out of the back.

'Hello, there,' he said, shaking hands with me. 'How are you?'

'Swell,' I said.

'Ready, Ethel?'

'Yes, Sammy.' She turned to me. 'Call me tonight and let me know how you made out with Bergerman.'

'Yes, ma'am. But you'd better let me have your phone number.'

Lally helped her into the back of the car.

'It's in the book,' she said. 'It's one of the few Beverly Hills names you'll find in the book. And don't forget to call me.'

'No, ma'am, thank you. I won't.'

I was a little self-conscious that all this conversation was taking place before Lally, a little embarrassed. He didn't speak as they drove off.

I turned and went back into the court, to the bungalow, hoping Mona would not make too much of a scene, telling myself that meeting Mrs. Smithers was the thing I had been waiting for and that I was the luckiest guy in town, but not feeling any too good about it inside. I mean I didn't feel as good as if my test at Excelsior had been wonderful and they had signed me to a contract. This way, with Mrs. Smithers helping me, giving me money, making an appointment with an agent, made me a little ashamed, and that was what took the edge off my elation.

Still, I thought, you have to play ball to get anywhere. Even if anybody does find out about it they'll forget when I become a big star. . . .

Mona was talking to a girl when I went into the bungalow. It was Miss Hollingsworth, the fan-magazine writer. After Mona had introduced us, I said: 'I didn't have a chance to tell you she was coming. She phoned while you were at the market.'

'That's all right,' Mona said coldly. She was still thinking about Mrs. Smithers. 'I haven't got any story to give you,' she said to Miss Hollingsworth.

'Mrs. Smithers suggested I talk to you,' Miss Hollingsworth said. 'She thought – and so do I – that your angle on her party would be something different to write. An extra girl's impression of a swank Hollywood party, you know.'

'Yes – I know,' Mona said, 'but I can't give you a story.'

'Of course,' Miss Hollingsworth continued in the same tone, as if Mona had said nothing, 'it's a good break for an unknown girl, getting into a national magazine, with pictures and everything – you've got some pictures, haven't you?'

'Yes, I've got some pictures. But I'm not going to give you a story.'

'I think it's a good idea,' I said.

'No,' Mona said.

Miss Hollingsworth stared at her, frowning.

'Just because you're sore at me's no reason you should take it out on her,' I said to Mona.

'That's got nothing to do with it. I'm sorry,' she said. 'You'll just have to excuse me.'

'Well,' Miss Hollingsworth said, shrugging, 'if you won't, you won't. At least it's a novelty to meet an extra girl who refuses publicity.'

'I don't like fan magazines,' Mona said in a flat voice.

Miss Hollingsworth got up to go.

'I didn't start them,' she said, a little sarcastic. 'I only work for one. I'm sorry I bothered you. Good-bye.'

She turned and went out the door. I waited until I saw her pass the window, going down the court, and then I said:

'That was a hell of a thing to do.'

'It was your fault. You shouldn't have asked her to come here.'

'I didn't see any harm in it. I didn't know you felt that way about them.'

'Goddam 'em, I hate 'em,' she said, folding her arms. 'There ought to be a law against them. Printing all those goddam lies, all those goddam pictures of Crawford and Gaynor and Loy and Lombard and all the others beside their swimming pools and in specially made clothes and

telling about how they started at the bottom and rose to
fame and fortune – what do you think that does for all the
millions of other girls in this country – the millions of
waitresses and small-town girls?'

I had never seen her quite like this before, had never
heard that tone in her voice. It was a quiet tone, but it was
sharp as a needle. Her eyes were almost closed. It scared
me.

'Wait a minute,' I said.

'I'll tell you what it does,' she said. 'It makes them
discontented. They say to themselves: "If they did it, so can
I." And they come to this goddam town and starve to death.
Look at Dorothy. Where is she today? In Tehachapi – in
prison, her life ruined. Why? "If Crawford did it, so can I."
She should have married that radio salesman. Fan magazines, that's what. If she'd never read fan magazines – ' She
broke off and started sobbing, falling on the davenport.
'Damn, damn, damn, damn – ' she sobbed.

I knelt down beside her, not knowing what to do or say. I
could only look, not believing my eyes. I felt the way you
would if you were to see the Rock of Gibraltar being slowly
melted by rainfall.

'Mona, Mona, listen to me,' I said, putting my hands on
her shoulders, trying to turn her over. She pulled away from
me. I got up and brought her a glass of water. 'Here – drink
this,' I said.

She slowly turned over and I saw her eyes were red and
the tears were streaming down her cheeks. She tried to smile
at me.

'Drink this,' I said, handing her the glass.

She drank it.

'I'm sorry,' she said, sitting up, wiping her eyes with the heel of her hands, straightening her hair. 'Thank you for the water.'

'You want the rest of it?' I asked.

'No, thanks.'

I put the glass on the desk and when I turned back she was standing up.

'Don't you want some lunch?' she asked.

'Let's go out for lunch,' I said. 'Let's go to the Derby.'

'Are you crazy?' she finally managed to say. 'I thought that was your pet hate.'

I shook my head, smiling.

'Not any more. Look,' I said, holding up the hundred-dollar bill Mrs. Smithers had given me. 'The worm has turned.'

For a moment she was too surprised to utter a word. She came over and inspected the bill.

'I know your folks didn't send you that much. Where'd you get it?'

'Never mind where I got it. I got it and that's all you need to know. Now I can pay my part of the rent and food and have some left over. And I got a date with an agent this afternoon, too.'

She nodded, taking a deep breath.

'She's certainly a fast worker,' she said, going into the kitchen, taking the groceries out of the shopping-bag.

'It's just a loan,' I said. 'She's interested in my career, that's all.'

'That's a new name for it. That's a six-letter word. The thing she's interested in's only got five letters.'

'What do you mean?' I asked.

'Skip it. So she gave you a hundred bucks and made a date with an agent for you. Well, when you get to the top I hope you won't forget your humble beginnings. Drop around occasionally with a ham sandwich.'

I took the bottle of milk out of her hand and put it on the ice-box.

'Don't let's be like this,' I said. 'Let's go somewhere for lunch. Let's go see people.'

'Smithers is a miracle woman,' she said, shaking her head. 'She's certainly got you over your fixations in short order. It didn't take her long. It didn't take her long to get your self-respect either.'

'Self-respect! Self-respect in the movies is the biggest liability you can have. I haven't got any after last night.'

'What happened last night?' she asked suddenly.

'I mean about that nigger kissing Helga Carruthers. When I let him get away with that I knew I didn't have any self-respect. But if it'd been my sister – '

'There you-all go again,' she said, kidding my accent.

'I can't help it if I'm from the South, can I?' I said. 'I'm trying to get rid of my accent.'

'I didn't mean that. I meant you were being professionally Southern again. Jesus, stop being that way.'

She was beginning to make me sore.

'I'm not professionally Southern,' I replied. 'I don't like 'em any more than you do. If I had my way I'd wipe the

47

whole South right off the map. They're stupid and ignorant and illiterate and live in the Dark Ages. I know that. But white women don't go around necking niggers. Not nice white women. But the hell with all this. I haven't got any self-respect and that's that. Will you go out to lunch with me?'

'On her money? Not on your sweet life.'

'Won't you please understand the woman's only trying to help me?' I asked desperately.

'Well,' she said, 'as far as I'm concerned, the subject is closed. I don't want to hear any more about Mrs. Smithers. After she lays you once or twice she'll drop you so fast your head'll ache for a week. Go ahead and let her help you – but don't come crawling back here looking for a place to sleep and something to eat.'

'All right, for Christ's sake, I won't go out with her,' I said.

'Please – ' she said wearily.

'Do you mind if I stay here and have lunch?'

'Help yourself,' she said.

...*chapter seven*

That afternoon I went out to see Stanley Bergerman. His office was on the county strip on Sunset Boulevard where it curved into Beverly Hills. The girl at the desk said he was expecting me and would I mind waiting a few minutes.

'No, ma'am,' I said, sitting down in the waiting-room.

Why can't all the girls who work for agents be that nice? I thought.

In a few minutes Mr. Bergerman came out, shook hands with me, and asked me to come into his office. I put my scrapbook on his desk and sat down.

'Mrs. Smithers seems to think you've got possibilities,' he said.

'I hope so,' I answered.

He looked at me, frowning.

'You're from the South.'

'Yes, sir – from Georgia.'

He lighted a cigarette thoughtfully, taking a long time, and I knew from the look on his face that whatever interest he might have had in me was now gone.

'That's quite an accent you have. That makes it bad.'

'I didn't think it was that noticeable.'

'It's thick enough to cut with a board,' he said. 'No wonder you've had trouble getting into pictures.'

I told him about the Little Theater back home and about Mr. Balter bringing me out and making the test and how nothing had ever come of it – and that I had finally started doing extra work because I thought that was the way to get experience. I showed him the scrapbook, with all my performances written up in the newspaper; and the new stories, the ones my mother had sent me since I had been in Hollywood about how well I was doing, about the stars I was hobnobbing with.

'Do you really know all these people?' he asked.

'No,' I said. 'I used all their names in letters I wrote to my mother, just to prove to her I was getting along all right, but she believed them and gave them to a friend of hers who works on a newspaper and he printed them. I was scared at first – I only did it because my mother kept writing me to come home and I thought I could prove to her that Hollywood was the place for me.'

'I understand,' he said.

'Now you see why I've got to get into pictures. Everybody in my home town thinks I'm practically a star now, and if I don't get into pictures pretty soon where they can see me, they are going to think something is funny.'

He nodded and put down his cigarette, looking at me.

'You've certainly got all the physical equipment. I don't think I ever saw any youngster as handsome – and if this was in the days of silent pictures I'd have you a star within a week. But not now, not with sound. I'd like to handle you if you could do something about that accent.'

'But I'm a good actor, Mr. Bergerman,' I said, trying to fight off that helpless feeling that was coming over me again, that panicky feeling. 'I know I can make good if I had the chance.'

'And you've got no experience either.'

'How can I get experience if nobody will give me a chance?' I asked.

'I've asked them that same question a thousand times,' he said. 'There's no answer for it. The thing for you to do is work on that accent. Then, if you are determined on a picture career, go to New York and get in a play. That's the best way to beat this game – make 'em come after you. When you go after them you're licked before you start.'

'Gary Cooper did it.'

He shrugged.

'One in a thousand. One in twenty thousand.'

'Well,' I said, picking up my scrapbook, 'if he did it, so can I. I'll go on being an extra until my chance comes.' I stood up. 'Thank you for letting me take up your time.'

'That's all right, Carston. I'm sorry I can't do something for you. But it's better that you know the truth about this.'

'I don't mind the truth.'

'That's fine,' he said. 'Of course, I'm not the best man in the world to advise you, but I can't help thinking you'd be much happier back home being a star in the Little Theater, where all your friends are.'

'I'm not going home,' I told him. 'I'm here to stay.'

I shook hands with him.

'Thanks again, Mr. Bergerman.'

'If I can do anything else to help you – if you'll work on that accent – '

'Thanks,' I said, going out, going downstairs, and getting into Mona's car.

It was late afternoon and the sun was setting somewhere behind Beverly Hills, where all the famous movie stars lived. As I turned around on Sunset and started back, I could see Los Angeles and Hollywood spread below me.

One of these days, I thought . . .

I put the car in the garage next to the bungalow court and went to the market. I felt much better now than when I had left Bergerman's office. I had thought over what he said and although I knew he was right (other people had told me the same thing), more than ever now my mind was made up to stay in Hollywood. I was going to do something in pictures yet, something big, accent or no accent.

'I'll die before I go back home,' I said to myself.

'Hello, there,' said Abie, the cashier at the market. 'What's that you got under your arm?'

'My scrapbook,' I replied.

He grinned, pointing to Les, the clerk, who was standing by the cash register.

'Him, too,' he said. 'He's got one. Hey, Les, tell Ralph about the time you was with Le Gallienne – '

'Don't mind him,' Les said to me. 'It's a case of sour grapes. He's a goddam bourgeois.'

'Yeah?' Abie said, patting his fat stomach. 'I notice none of you proletariat's got one of these. Goddam right,' he said to me. 'Difference between a red and a capitalist's a fat stomach.'

I smiled. Abie was always kidding everybody, but he was one of the best guys I ever met. He was boss of the market and it was probably the only market in Hollywood where an extra could get credit.

'How much do we owe?' I asked him.

'Plenty,' he said. 'Why?'

'I want to pay you,' I said, laying the hundred-dollar bill on the counter.

'Holy jumping Jesus,' he said, picking up the bill, holding it up to the light. 'You must've signed a contract with Metro or somebody.'

'Not yet, I haven't. Can you change it?'

'Sure,' he said, putting the bill on the cash register, looking in his account book. 'Eight bucks sixteen. That includes the dollar cash for gasoline.'

'Mona got some stuff at noon,' I said. 'Is that included too?'

'No,' he said, looking through the tickets. He found the ticket and added the whole thing up. 'Nine twenty-five right on the nose.'

He counted out the change and handed it to me, marking the account paid.

'Look here, kid,' he said. 'This is on the level? Where'd you get this much dough?'

'It's on the level, all right. I didn't steal it.'

'Okay. Don't ever pull any rough stuff to get dough to pay me. I'm the guy to worry about the bill, not you.'

'Thanks, Abie,' I said. I put the change in my pocket and walked back to the court. I stopped in the manager's office and paid a month's rent in advance, twenty-five dollars. Then I went back to the bungalow.

53

Mona was writing a letter. She had changed her dress and had removed all the make-up from her face, looking like a young housewife in one of those ads in a woman's magazine.

'So soon? What happened?'

I told her what Bergerman had said.

'Well,' she said, 'that's better than stalling you along like most of these agents do. But don't let him discourage you. You're not discouraged, are you?'

'No,' I said, handing her the receipt for the rent.

'What's this?' she asked.

'I paid a month's rent in advance out of that hundred dollars. Also, I paid Abie off, too.'

The shadow of a frown crossed her face, and then she smiled.

'Well,' she said slowly, 'there's no reason why I should worry about my self-respect either. You're sweet, Ralph.'

'Say, I'm glad to be able to do it. You've been carrying the load long enough – '

'You're sweet anyway. Don't you want to take a bath? Go on – make you feel better.'

'I will. I want to get rid of this first,' I said, holding up the scrapbook, going into the kitchen.

I was tearing the sheets out, tearing them into bits, and putting them in the garbage can when Mona came running in.

'Ralph! What are you doing? Oh – ' she exclaimed when she saw what was happening. 'You shouldn't have done that. Not that.'

'Why?' I asked calmly, putting the last pieces into the can. 'I've got no further use for it.'

54

'Just the same – Well, it's no good crying about it now.'

'I'll say it isn't.'

'That's a symbol,' she said quietly, looking at the garbage can.

'A what?'

'Nothing,' she said. 'Nothing – ' looking at me with a steady gaze. Her eyes were blue. Even in the semidarkness of the kitchen I could see that. This surprised me; not that her eyes were blue, but that she had any eyes at all. I'd never paid any attention before.

I walked out of the kitchen suddenly, going upstairs to take a bath, not saying anything at all.

...chapter
eight

After dinner, after the Lum and Abner program, I went across the street to the drug store and called Mrs. Smithers. She said she was waiting to hear from me, that she had talked to Bergerman and was very sorry that he hadn't been able to help me, but that in no way must I let that discourage me. I told her I wasn't discouraged, that with her to help me I was more confident than ever.

'That's fine,' she said. 'Did you get the new suit yet?'

'Why, no, ma'am,' I said. 'I haven't had time.'

'Well, no matter. I want to see you tonight.'

'Mrs. Smithers – '

'Tush, tush. I'll be in front of your place at ten thirty.'

She hung up before I could finish what I was trying to say. I didn't want to leave Mona. I couldn't forget the picture of her lying on the davenport sobbing.

'Now I am in a jam,' I said to myself.

Tommy Mosher was talking to Mona when I got back. He was a former football player who was now a third assistant director for Meteor. He lived in the same court, a couple of bungalows away.

'Hi, Gawguh,' he said to me.

'Hello, Tommy,' I said. I'd seen him around a lot, but he

was no particular friend of mine. I always felt that he could have helped both Mona and me get work if he'd really wanted to. Other assistant directors always managed to help people they knew.

'I'm trying to talk Mona into going out with me tonight,' he said.

'Why don't you, Mona? Do you good.'

She looked at me curiously.

'Have you got a date?'

'What makes you think I've got a date?'

'The reasons are obvious,' she said, still looking at me. – 'All right, Tommy,' she said after a moment. 'I'd be delighted.'

'Good – I'll change clothes and come by in thirty minutes. So long Gawguh,' he said, going out.

I walked over and changed stations on the radio, getting an orchestra, Jan Garber's. Out of the corner of my eye I could see Mona was watching me closely.

'I hope you have a good time,' I said finally.

'Oh, don't worry about that,' she replied. 'I'll have a good time. I'll have a hell of a time. Yes, sir. And I hope you have a good time too.'

'What makes you think I'm going anywhere?'

'Nuts,' she said, going upstairs, slamming the door of her bedroom.

At ten thirty Mrs. Smithers picked me up. Lally was not with her.

'Get in, dear boy,' she said, opening the door for me herself. 'All right, Walter,' she said to the driver.

I sat down beside her, pretending in that moment that this

was my car and I was being driven to the Carthay Circle to
see the première of my new picture.

'How are you, dear boy?' she asked, putting her hand on
my leg. 'Forget what happened this afternoon. That was
only the beginning.'

'I've forgotten it,' I said. 'As long as you've got faith in
me, I'm not worried.'

'Don't bother your pretty head with it. Just leave everything to me. I've got grand plans for you.'

'Thank you, ma'am. . . . Where's Lally?'

'This is Thursday night,' she said.

I looked at her, not understanding.

'Thursday night?'

'You dear boy,' she said, laughing. 'This is charming –
charming. It's his night off.'

'Oh – ' I said.

The driver turned off Vine on to Sunset, going west.
Hollywood, here I am, I thought, my heart pounding with
excitement; this is where I belong, this is my destiny, this big
car and this chauffeur and this rich woman by my side are
not strange – all this is an omen as infallible as those funnel-
shaped black clouds back home are omens and everybody
knows what surely will happen. That's not right, I thought
quickly, a little frightened that I had likened what was going
to happen to me to what was going to happen to a town that
saw one of those clouds approaching; that's not what I mean
to think, I thought. . . .

We crossed La Brea where the Chaplin studios were, dark
and deserted. 'I know what you went through, Charlie,' I
said to myself.

'Why so pensive? You promised me you wouldn't worry.'

'I'm not worrying – I feel wonderful. Where're we going?'

'To the Trocadero. Have you ever been to the Troc?'

'No, ma'am – I've never been to any of those places.'

'Good,' she said. 'I want to show you Hollywood night life myself.'

They all knew Mrs. Smithers at the Trocadero, the footman, the doorman, the hat-check girl, the head waiter – everybody.

'Good evening, Mrs. Smithers,' the head waiter said, smiling. 'Are you having dinner?'

'Just a drink or two, thank you,' she said, leading me downstairs to the bar. The bar was pretty crowded, and as we went down the steps, they all turned, looking at us. It was a fine entrance. I had had enough experience in the Little Theater to appreciate this.

The guy who put those steps there knew what he was doing, I thought.

Mrs. Smithers nodded to several people, and a waiter led us into one of the booths.

'I'll have Ballantine's and soda,' she said. 'What'll you have?'

'I don't care,' I said, not knowing exactly what to order.

'Two,' she said to the waiter.

I looked around. Most of the people were still staring at us. Several of them waved to Mrs. Smithers, who waved back.

'There's Barbara Stanwyck and Robert Taylor,' she whispered, leaning over.

'Where?'

'Right over there,' she said, waving to them.

They waved back, nodding.

'See them?'

'Yes,' I said. 'I don't think he's so good.'

She patted my hand under the table.

'Don't be jealous, now. Your chance'll come. He's a nice boy.'

'He may be a very nice boy,' I said, 'but I don't think he's such a hot actor. He's not as good as Spencer Tracy or Paul Muni. Do you know them?'

'Yes, yes – I know them.'

The waiter brought the drinks and a bowl of parched corn. I took a couple of swallows of my drink, not wanting it, but being polite. Everybody in the bar was talking. They were pretty loud.

'This is one of the show places of Hollywood,' Mrs. Smithers said.

'I know. I've read about it in the fan magazines,' I said, telling myself that when I got to be a star I'd be different and do what drinking I had to do at home.

'See that little fellow over there?' she said, pointing to a table. 'The one standing up?'

'Yes.'

'That's Sidney Skolsky, the columnist.'

Skolsky turned around at that moment and she waved to him. He waved back, looking at me curiously.

'He's surprised Sammy isn't with me,' she said.

I took a few more swallows of the drink. I was not excited any more about the Trocadero. All that was gone. I was

beginning to wonder where Mona was and what she was
doing; and the old feeling about the celebrities and the
Brown Derby and the Trocadero and places like that was
coming back. I thought I had got over my hatred for them,
but I was wrong. I hated everybody present for no reason
except that they were successful. All along I had felt that an
extra, an unknown, had no business coming to places like
these – and now I knew I was right. I had absolutely no
business here.

I said so to Mrs. Smithers. She was very much surprised.
She asked me what I meant and I tried to explain.

'Why – that's silly,' she said, laughing. 'That's only your
inferiority complex.'

'I don't care what it is,' I said. 'I'm miserable and let's
leave before I go over there and punch Robert Taylor in the
nose and tear this joint to pieces.'

'My, my!' she said, still laughing. 'You have got an
inferiority complex. You've got the wrong perspective, dear
boy. None of these people know you. They don't know
you're only an extra. Don't you see that? As far as they are
concerned, you might be a celebrity too – you might be a
big-game hunter or a transatlantic flyer – '

'I wish I were a transatlantic flyer,' I said. 'I wish I were
in the middle of the ocean right now.'

'Here, here – that's no way to talk. Is that what one drink
does to you?'

'The drink's got nothing to do with it,' I said.

She looked at me, frowning. I knew she was annoyed, but
I didn't care. It made me sore, sitting here looking at Robert
Taylor, the biggest star in the pictures, trying to figure out

what he had that put him where he was, telling myself that I was as good as he was and that, goddam it, one of these days. . . . 'All right,' she said, finishing her drink. 'Would you like to go to the Clover Club or the Hawaiian Paradise or Sebastian's – '

'Why do we have to go anywhere? Why can't we just ride around in the car and talk?'

She laughed.

'How quaint!' she exclaimed, motioning for the waiter.

I gave the waiter three one-dollar bills, telling him to keep the change, and we started for the stairs, Mrs. Smithers waving good-bye to all the people she knew. At the head of the stairs she met a man in a tuxedo and greeted him warmly. I remembered him from her party the night before as the one who had been singing, but I didn't know his name.

'Here, Ralph,' she said, catching me by the arm. 'I want you to meet a friend of mine. Ralph Carston, this is Arthur Wharton – the finest motion-picture director in the world.'

Wharton bowed low to Mrs. Smithers, kissing her hand.

'Smithers, you always say the perfect thing. – Hello, Carston,' he said to me, shaking hands.

'This is my new protégé, Arthur.'

Wharton winked at me.

'You're in good hands, Carston – the best. What do you do?'

'He's an actor,' Mrs. Smithers said. 'He's the new big star of 1938. Aren't you?' she asked me.

'I hope so,' I replied, self-conscious. She wasn't kidding when she said Arthur Wharton was the finest director in the world. I had heard of him, even back home. He was as important as De Mille.

'Arthur,' she said, 'you've simply got to give this boy a test.'

'Well, now – ' Wharton said, his face clouding a little.

'You've simply got to,' she insisted.

'Tell you what, Carston,' he said to me. 'You call me tomorrow at the studio. I'll see what I can do.'

'Thank you, Mr. Wharton,' I said. I was so surprised at meeting him, at all this that was happening, I didn't know what else to say.

'You're a dear, Arthur. I'll see you Sunday, won't I? Sunday afternoon?'

'Of course you will – of course. Good night.'

He went down the steps to the bar.

'You see?' she said to me.

'I see,' I said.

Outside we had to wait about five minutes while an attendant at the parking lot went to get Walter, the chauffeur, who was off at one of the other bars in the neighborhood. A dozen people went into the Trocadero in the time we stood there, and Mrs. Smithers knew at least ten of them, greeting them as if they all had just got back from a long trip round the world. One of the women was so drunk it took two men to get her inside without falling. Mrs. Smithers told me who she was, the wife of some well-known producer, and I thought: I'll remember that and blackmail him if the Wharton thing falls through, but the next moment I'd forgotten who she said it was.

Walter finally brought the car up, stopping it across the

pavement, getting out, and helping us in. He apologized for keeping her waiting, saying he thought she'd be in there at least an hour.

'Ralph's bored,' she said. 'We're going to ride around. Tell Walter where you want to go,' she said.

'I don't care,' I replied. 'Anywhere.'

'Would you like to go to my house?'

'Sure. That'd be fine.'

'Turn around, Walter,' she said. 'We're going home.'

I couldn't get over meeting Arthur Wharton. He was one man in Hollywood who had the power to do anything he wanted to. He had made more stars than you could count on the fingers of both hands. If he only likes me, I thought . . .

We were alone in the house. The servants were out and Mrs. Smithers brought in a tray of drinks herself, putting them on the piano. She came over and put her arms around me and kissed me on the mouth. I was not surprised.

'Wouldn't you like to go upstairs where it'd be more comfortable?' she asked.

'Sure,' I said.

'Bring the tray and follow me.'

I picked up the tray, following her upstairs into her bedroom. There was one small light burning on the table by the bed. I put the tray on a table, and as I straightened up she grabbed me and kissed me again. This time I put my arms around her.

'That's better,' she said in a low tone. 'Now you excuse me for a moment while I get into something comfortable. Mix a drink.'

She disappeared into a little room and was back in a minute or two, wearing a white silk négligé. She had on so much perfume it hurt my eyes.

'There,' she said, taking the drink, tasting it. 'Come – let's sit here.'

I sat down beside her on the couch.

I'll play a scene like this someday, I thought. A thousand of them. . . .

'What'll we talk about?' she said.

'Anything. Anything at all.'

'Let's talk about you. You won't forget me when you become a star, will you?'

'Of course not,' I said.

'You'll have all the women in America at your feet – '

'That still won't make any difference.'

'What's the first thing you're going to do after you become a star?'

'Go home,' I said.

'That's not what I mean. You can go home any time.'

'Oh, no, I can't,' I said. 'That's the one thing I can't do. All the guys laughed at me when I came out here. I'm not going back there until I'm the biggest star in pictures.'

'Your girl believes in you though, doesn't she?'

'I haven't got a girl.'

'No girl?'

'No.'

'What about the one you live with?'

'Mona? She's not my girl. She's more of a sister.'

'Or mother perhaps?'

'Something like that,' I said.

She held up her glass to my lips and I took a sip of the Scotch and soda.

'How old are you?'

'Twenty-three.'

'You're a big boy for twenty-three.'

'Well, I spent most of my life on a farm. You have to be big to be a farmer.'

Neither of us said anything for a moment.

'Did anybody ever tell you you were handsome?' she asked.

'No, ma'am,' I said, feeling my cheeks get hot.

'You are. You're the handsomest boy I've seen in my life.'

I looked away, out the window. She put her drink on the tray and leaned over, her body touching mine.

'And I'm crazy about you,' she said. 'I'm mad about you.'

Before I could do or say anything she took my head in her hands, kissing me all over the face and eyes and biting my ear. I finally pushed her away, standing up. She pulled me down beside her again.

'Please – please – ' she said. 'Don't you like me a little?'

'Of course, I like you. I like you a lot. Why shouldn't I? You've been nice to me.'

'Kiss me,' she said. 'Touch me. Hit me. Anything.'

I kissed her on the lips.

'Not like that,' she said. 'Not like that. Like this.'

She grabbed my head between her hands again and kissed me furiously all over the face, biting my chin. I put my hand on her shoulders, not pushing her away this time, just holding her off. I could feel the wrinkles of skin between my fingers. It made me a little sick. She was as old as my mother.

She kept on kissing me, finally, unbuttoning my shirt, kissing me on the chest. In a moment she stopped, looking at me, the muscles in her face quivering, her lower lip between her teeth. I had never seen anybody look like this before. I was scared.

'I've got to get out of here,' I told myself.

Suddenly she reached over and slapped me hard in the face. I stood up, trembling like a leaf.

'If you were a man I'd kick your teeth out,' I said.

She stood up beside me, her hands on her hips, sticking out her chin.

'Go on – hit me. Hit me,' she said.

'I'm not going to hit you,' I said. 'I'm going home.'

'Go home, you stupid son of a bitch, you stupid farmer son of a bitch, you hick-town farmer son of a bitch, you dumb-ox son of a bitch – '

I walked out, leaving her standing, still swearing at me.

...*chapter nine*

The next morning it was raining. I waked up and saw the rain and turned over and went back to sleep again, feeling very cozy. When I waked up again some man was standing by the davenport looking down at me, a total stranger. He was about thirty-five and his clothes were wrinkled, as if he had slept in them, and smelled of liquor.

'Who're you?' he said.

'Who're you?' I asked, sitting up, kicking the blankets off, buttoning the coat of my pajamas.

'Do you live here?' he asked.

'Certainly I live here,' I said.

He frowned, looking around the room.

'Where is this place? Am I in Hollywood?'

'Certainly, you're in Hollywood,' I said. He's still drunk I thought. I looked around to see if the door was open, thinking he may have strayed in. The door was closed.

'How'd you get in here?' I asked.

'I'll be goddamed if I know,' he said, shaking his head. 'All I know is I slept up there.'

He pointed up towards Mona's room. I got up, slipping on my shoes.

'I hope I didn't rob you of your bed,' he said.

'It's not my bed,' I answered.

He sat down in the chair and lighted a cigarette.

'Somebody must've brought me here,' he said. 'Maybe I can remember – '

I stood there wondering whether to throw him out, and then I thought I'd see what Mona had to say about it. If he had slept with her she should know him, I thought. I went upstairs and looked into the bedroom. Mona was not there.

'Did Mona bring you here?' I asked him, coming downstairs.

His face lighted up.

'Is this Mona's place?'

'Yes.'

'I guess she did,' he said, apologetically. 'I was on a party with her last night and I got stinking – or can you tell that?'

'Oh, no,' I said.

He pushed himself out of the chair, coming to me with his hand stretched out.

'My name's Hill – Johnny Hill.'

I took his hand.

'I hope you're not sore,' he said.

'I'm not sore.'

'Christ, I got stinking,' he said.

'Sit down,' I told him. 'I don't know where Mona is. Didn't she come home with you?'

'I'll be goddamed if I know. She must have. I didn't just wander in here accidentally, because I've never been here before. I couldn't very well wander in a place I'd never seen before, could I?'

'Not very well,' I said.

69

'Are you in pictures?'

'Yes.'

'What studio?'

'I'm an extra.'

'Oh,' he said. Then: 'Where do you suppose Mona is?'

'I don't know.'

'She owes me an explanation,' he said. 'The idea of bringing me home with her and then taking a powder.'

'Don't you remember anything at all? Don't you remember whether you went to bed with her?'

'I don't remember a thing – my mind's a gorgeous blank. Christ,' he exclaimed, 'maybe she did go to bed with me. Wouldn't that be awful to forget a thing like that? You haven't got a drink, have you?'

'No. I'll fix some coffee for you if you want it.'

'Would you? Say, that'd be swell.'

I went into the kitchen. I didn't especially like him, but I thought he was a friend of Mona's and for that reason I should put up with him. Besides, I wanted coffee myself. He came in and stood by the stove.

'Christ – I got stinking last night.'

'You told me that,' I said.

He seemed surprised.

'Did I? Sorry. I quit my job yesterday and I was celebrating.'

'That's a funny thing to celebrate,' I said.

'No, it wasn't. – Have you got a phone?' he asked suddenly.

'Right in there,' I said, pointing.

He went in and dialled a number.

'I want to speak to Marc Lachmann,' he said. 'Hello, Lorna? This is Johnny. I wanna talk to Marc. . . . Where is he – on the lot? . . . No, that's all right. I just wanted to be sure I called him yesterday and quit. Did I? . . . That's fine. Just so I did. So long. . . .'

He came back into the kitchen. I poured him a cup of coffee.

'I wanted to check on that,' he said. 'I quit yesterday.'

'I heard you. You in the movies?'

'Publicity. I worked for Universal. I quit yesterday.' He sipped his coffee. 'You know why I quit?'

'No.'

He reached for his wallet and took out a small newspaper clipping.

'This was in the Los Angeles *Times* yesterday,' he said. 'This is from the movie column in that great reactionary journal. Listen: "The German Consul, incensed at final scenes in *The Road Back*" – that's one of our big pictures – "incensed at final scenes in *The Road Back*, showing German youngsters being drilled as soldiers, has induced Universal to revise the film's ending. At the same time the studio will try to work in some more love interest."' He took a few more sips of his coffee, looking at me. 'That's why I quit,' he said. 'Wouldn't you?'

'I don't know,' I said. 'I don't see anything in that article to make you quit.'

'You don't? Haven't you seen any of those pictures in *Life* or *Fortune* about all the German youth being drilled in uniforms with guns and wearing signs across their breasts: "We were Born to Die for Hitler"?'

71

'I don't believe so,' I said.

'Well, it's true anyway. That Hitler's going to start another war and why should the German Consul get his bowels in an uproar because we show German kids drilling? I didn't get sore about that, you understand, because the German Consul's bowels are always in an uproar about something. What I got sore about was the studio letting him tell 'em where to get off. I know what I'd told him. But none of these studios've got any guts. They're all yellow. Why, one time I was working at Metro – '

He stopped, looking behind him. It was Mona.

'Hello,' she said. 'I see you're already acquainted.'

'Sure,' Johnny said, getting up. 'Sure, we're old friends. Have some coffee?'

'Thanks,' she said, looking at me.

I got a cup and poured her some.

'Was he here last night when we came in?' Johnny asked.

'Yes.'

'I don't remember seeing him. How was it I didn't see him?'

'In your condition you couldn't see anything,' she said.

'How'd you happen to bring me home with you? Not,' he said, 'that I'm questioning your impeccable taste. I'm just curious.'

'The chief reason,' Mona said, speaking to him, but looking straight at me, 'is that you were in the cab with me and you couldn't remember where you lived yourself, so I gave you my bed and went over to the bungalow across the court – the one Dorothy, a friend of mine, used to have –

72

and crawled through the window and spent the night. Does that clear up everything?'

'Beautifully,' he said. 'Beautifully.'

I felt better too. All the time I was talking to Johnny I was wondering . . .

'Feeling better?' she asked him – 'or do you still hate Universal?'

'I hate 'em all,' he said. 'How'd you know about Universal?'

'You only told me the story twenty times.'

'Did I?'

'What happened to the guy you went with – Tommy Mosher?' I asked Mona.

'He left about one o'clock. He had an early call.'

Johnny pulled out a chair for Mona, asking: 'How's about me moving in here with you?'

'That'd make it a trifle crowded. Besides, you overlook the fact that we're extras. We might contaminate you.'

'That's not so ghastly. I'm going to be an extra myself. Or did I also reveal that secret to you last night?'

Mona laughed.

'No – that's one you kept.'

'Well, I am,' he said. 'I've been waiting to be an extra for years and now I'm going to.'

'If you insist on starving. I suppose that's as good a way as any,' Mona said.

'On the level,' he said. 'Oh, I don't mean extra work as a career – I'm going to write a novel about extras in the movies. How they live, what they think – you know, there's a big field there.'

73

He was very serious.

'All the tragedy and heart-break in this goddam four-flushing town, all the viciousness and cruelty – '

I can give you some material for that, Johnny, I thought.

'That side of Hollywood's never been told. All you ever read about Hollywood is the waitress who gets a test and turns out to be a big shot. Like *A Star is Born.* That was a good picture and it'll make a lot of money. That was *a* true story, but not *the* true story, if you know what I mean.'

'I think I do,' Mona said.

'The true story of this town concerns people like you – a girl like you and a boy like him. Maybe I'll put you two in a book.'

'No kidding,' Mona said.

'Why not?' he said. 'The very fact that you're an average boy and girl, the average extras, makes it all the more the reason. You're symbolic of the twenty thousand extras in Hollywood. Understand, I don't think I've got any special talent for novel-writing – not as much as the novelists have who've been out here. It's only that I think they've missed a good net. Hilton could have written it, Hammett, Hecht, Fowler – although he tried once with Mack Sennett and muffed it – and of course the old master, Dr. Hemingway, who could have done it better than anybody, but who's too goddam busy saving Spanish democracy to worry about a boy and girl in Hollywood. The trouble with those writers is they move to Malibu beach and into mansions at Bel-Air and run around with Mr. and Mrs. Richbitch's society and get to see the wrong side of it. That's like looking at something through the wrong end of the telescope – How's that for a speech from a guy who's got a roaring hangover?'

'Good,' said Mona. 'You ought to hire a hall.'

'I guess I should, at that,' he said, grinning. 'Well,' he added, getting up, 'I guess I'll take this beautiful brain and this roaring hangover out into the rain. Thanks for everything, and you must let me put you to bed some night. I'm going down now and picket the German Consul.'

He shook hands with both of us and walked out.

'A good guy,' Mona said, watching him go. 'Give you the shirt off his back.'

'He scared hell out of me when I waked up and saw him standing by the davenport,' I said.

'I thought I could get back over here before he woke up,' Mona said. 'I would have told you about it last night, but you were sleeping so peacefully I didn't want to wake you up.'

'I got in early,' I said.

'It must have been a hell of a party while it lasted. Your face looks like you'd been wrassling with a panther.'

I went into the living-room and looked in the mirror that hung over the desk. My cheeks and chin were bruised from where Mrs. Smithers had kissed me. In the mirror I could see Mona was standing behind me, smiling.

'I couldn't help it,' I said, turning around.

'You don't have to apologize to me,' she said. 'What the hell – you do whatever you please. Only I'm disappointed in you, that's all. You've always taken my advice about everything but this. I told you what she was.'

'I know that now,' I said, feeling miserable. 'I thought she was serious about helping me get a break.'

Mona did not say anything, looking at me scornfully. I knew she was right in everything she had said, it had turned out exactly as she had predicted. I felt so guilty about it there was nothing I could say.

'I'll go upstairs while you dress,' she said.

'Mona – ' I said.

She did not answer me, continuing up the stairs, going into her room, shutting the door.

When I finished dressing I went upstairs to the bathroom to wash my teeth. I knocked on the door and told her to come on downstairs and be sociable. She said she'd be down in a minute.

It was still raining. That raggledy palm tree in the middle of the court was more raggledy and forlorn than ever. Nothing looks any more forlorn in the rain than a Hollywood palm tree, I thought. A fog was coming in from the sea, and you could not see very far beyond the bungalows across the court. I watched Mrs. Anstruther, the court manager, go in Dorothy's old bungalow with a man and a woman, showing it to them. Poor Dorothy, I thought, feeling sorry for her now, taking back all those names I had called her. Poor Dorothy, I thought. Hollywood certainly gave you a lousy deal. You never would have stolen that stuff if you could have got work in pictures. 'Mona is right about the fan magazines,' I told myself. 'That's what brought Dorothy out here too – and now look at her.' Then, for no reason, I started thinking about Mrs. Smithers and the Trocadero and I remembered something that gave me such a thrill I could have shouted.

Arthur Wharton had asked me to call him.

I looked up the number of the studio and called his office. His secretary asked me who was talking and I had to spell my name twice before she got it. She said she'd see if he was in, and a moment later she said she was sorry, he was tied up in conference and would I write him a letter explaining what I wanted?

'He asked me to call him,' I said.

'Just a moment,' she said.

I wondered if this was going to fall through too.

'I'm sorry,' the secretary said, picking up the phone again. 'Mr. Wharton doesn't remember – '

'Listen,' I said, almost begging her. 'Just say I'm the boy he met with Mrs. Smithers last night in the Trocadero. He promised me a test.'

'Hold the phone,' she said again, a note of irritation in her voice.

'He'll remember me now,' I thought.

'Hello,' the secretary said. 'Mr. Wharton says he remembers you and that he's dreadfully sorry, but that he's going out of town for a long vacation and that he'll be glad to see you when he gets back.'

'When will that be?' I managed to ask.

'In three or four months,' she said.

'Thank you,' I said, hanging up, looking out the window at the raggledy palm tree. . . .

'Who was that on the phone?' Mona asked.

'Nobody,' I said, going over to the window. 'A friend of mine.'

'It sounded like it,' she said. 'I wish you could have heard your voice. You sounded like somebody about to be hanged.' She came over and stood beside me. 'Who was it.'

'Nobody, I told you,' I said, walking back to the desk.

'But I heard you say you met him last night when you were with Mrs. Smithers.'

'Goddam it, let me alone,' I said.

She walked over now and stood directly in front of me.

'I'm not trying to pry into your business, Ralph,' she said quietly. 'I'm only trying to keep you from being hurt. You're entirely too trusting. Don't you see you're only laying yourself wide open for these people to break your heart?'

'They're not breaking my heart,' I said. 'One of these days I'll show them. I'll be the biggest star of them all before I'm through.'

'There, that's more like it,' she said, smiling. 'Don't get that dauber down.'

The phone rang and she answered it. When she heard the voice at the other end, her face grew grim.

'For you,' she said, holding out the receiver.

I took it, wondering who it could be.

'Good morning, you dear boy – and how are you this awful day?'

'I'm all right,' I said, trying to make up my mind what I should do.

'You aren't angry with me, are you?'

'No.'

78

'You mustn't be. I want you to go to lunch with me. To the Vendome.'

'I've had lunch.'

'Well, you can go with me and then we'll go shopping.'

'I've got to stay here and answer the phone.'

'Let that girl do that.'

'She's got a date. She's going out.'

'Then I'll have lunch and come by and see you.'

'But, Mrs. Smithers – '

'Good-bye, dear boy – I'll see you later.'

She hung up before I could think of something to say that would stop her.

'Is she coming here?' Mona asked.

'Yes.'

She looked at me for a full minute before she spoke.

'I guess there's no hope for you,' she said finally.

'She insisted,' I said. 'I don't want to see her.'

'Good God! Then why didn't you tell her that?'

'You don't know her. She won't take no for an answer.'

'Well, if you haven't got the guts enough to tell her where to get off, I have,' she said.

'I've got the guts,' I said. 'It's only that she's important and I don't want to make her sore at me. I've been worried all morning thinking she was sore about last night.'

'What happened last night?'

I told her the part about where she cursed me and I walked out on her.

'That's fine, that's marvellous,' Mona said. 'Why didn't you do that just now?'

'I've tried to tell you that I don't want to offend her.'

'Well, Jesus – you couldn't offend her much more than you did last night.'

'I didn't think then. I was sore.'

Mona laughed.

'You weren't sore. You were scared. That's why you walked out. You were scared.'

'I wasn't scared.'

'The hell you weren't. She tried to unbutton your pants and you got scared.'

I felt my cheeks burning.

'Haven't you ever done that with a woman? Haven't you?'

I was burning all over now.

'Are you a virgin? Tell me – are you a virgin?'

I still did not reply, turning my back on her, walking over to the window.

'Well, I'll be goddamed,' she said.

For the next hour or two we had very little to say to each other. The conversation was scattered, and what there was of it was very polite and strained, as if we were strangers and each was trying to impress the other with his good manners. I didn't know what was the matter with me. After last night, after the scene with Mrs. Smithers, I didn't care whether I ever saw her again; and yet here I was waiting for her to come. I didn't understand myself, except, as I had told Mona, I thought she might be able to help me. Not me alone, but Mona, too. I thought if I could get a break I might help Mona get one.

It was two o'clock when Mrs. Smithers arrived, wearing a Cellophane bag over her hat and a trench coat that made

her look twice as big as she was. I opened the door and let
her in.

'Hello, dear boy,' she said. 'Isn't this awful weather?'

Then she saw Mona and checked herself.

'Oh,' she said.

'Come in, come in,' Mona said. 'I was just going.'

She got up and went upstairs. I helped Mrs. Smithers off
with her trench coat and hat.

'There,' she said, 'that's better. Isn't this awful weather?'

'I like it for a change,' I said.

She looked around the room, wrinkling up the corners of
her eyes.

'My, my – it's comfortable here. Just like a regular love
nest.'

Mona came downstairs wearing a coat and no hat.

'You don't have to leave,' I said.

'Of course not,' Mrs. Smithers said. 'You can't go out
into this awful weather.'

'I don't think it's awful.'

She opened the door.

'I wish you wouldn't, Mona,' I said.

She went out, saying nothing else. I watched her pass the
window. It was still raining.

'I don't think she likes me,' Mrs. Smithers said. 'I think
she's jealous. In fact, I know she's jealous. Don't you think
she's jealous?'

'I don't know,' I said.

'What's the matter with you, dear boy? You act so
strangely. You're not still thinking of last night, are you?'

'Not any more.'

She sat down on the davenport.

'You mustn't let things like that upset you. I know I've got a nasty disposition, but I don't hold a grudge. The next minute I've forgotten all about it.'

'I've forgotten it too,' I said.

She looked at me thoughtfully as I sat down in the chair opposite her.

'I've been thinking a lot about last night,' she said. 'You aren't the kind of boy I thought you were at all. I mean you aren't the Hollywood type at all. You're very different.'

'Am I?'

We were quiet for a moment and did not talk. She lighted a cigarette and took a couple of puffs, studying me closely. I was ill at ease and self-conscious.

'Yes – you're different. Have you ever thought of getting married?'

'No, ma'am.'

'How does the idea strike you?'

'I've never thought about it. I've got other things on my mind.'

'Would you like to marry me?'

I looked at her. There was no emotion in her face, there was no expression at all. She knew what I was thinking.

'Why not? I've got loads of money and there's nothing wrong with you that money won't cure. I'm older than you – but what of that? Wouldn't you like to travel?'

'I suppose so,' I said quietly. I didn't feel any emotion either. She was the first woman who had ever said anything like that to me, and for that reason, if no other, I should have felt something. But I didn't.

'We could go away somewhere – Europe, the Far East – and forget all this.'

'I want to do something in pictures first,' I said, not wanting to refuse point-blank, not wanting to hurt her feelings.

'But it's such a struggle. I know what you're going through, I know what thousands of others are going through, and it isn't worth while. Haven't you ever thought of that?'

'No, ma'am,' I said. It was hard for me to believe this was the same woman I had been with last night, she was so calm and quiet.

'Well, if you wish, we could stay here. One sure way to get into pictures would be to marry me. I've no objection to my husband having a career, especially such a handsome husband. It wouldn't be fair to the rest of the women in the world.'

There was a knock on the door and I went over and opened it, thinking Mona had come back. It wasn't Mona. It was Sam Lally. He glared at me, saying nothing, and came in. I closed the door. Still saying nothing, he walked over to the chair and grabbed Mrs. Smithers's hat and trench coat and threw them into her lap.

'Come on,' he said.

'I'm not going,' she replied.

'One way or the other you are,' he said.

She threw the trench coat back at him. It struck him in the face and fell around his shoulders. He brushed it off and I could see the muscles in his jaws jumping.

'Sit down a minute, Lally,' I said.

'She's going and you keep quiet,' he said to me.

Mrs. Smithers laughed.

'He's always acting.' she said to me. 'He just loves situations like this.'

Lally took two strides across the floor and slapped her hard in the face, reaching down and grabbing her by the arms, trying to jerk her to her feet.

'I told you to come on,' he said, his voice excited.

He kept tugging at her, trying to get her up. I went over and shoved Lally away. He lost his balance, falling across the other end of the davenport.

'Cut it out,' I said.

'Yeah?' he snarled. He leaned over with his hand poised and before I could stop him he had slapped her twice more. 'You slut,' he said.

I hit Lally in the side of the head with my fist, and he looked at me, surprised, his lips pressed together. He pushed himself up slowly and I let him get on his feet before I hit him again. He swung at me, the blow glancing off my shoulder, and I wrapped my arms around him in a clinch, not wanting to hit him any more. I was bigger than he was, and stronger, and I did not want to take advantage of him.

'Cut it out,' I said, hugging him. 'Cut it out or you'll get hurt.'

He struggled to get loose, but I had a death hold on him and he couldn't budge me.

'Cut it out,' I said. I held him for a moment or two longer and then let him go, stepping back.

'Stop it, boys,' Mrs. Smithers said. It was the first word she had spoken since the fight started. 'Don't be so belligerent, Sammy. There's nothing between us.'

'You slut,' Lally said, not moving.

I looked over his shoulder at Mrs. Smithers. Her eyes were wild and she was grinning from ear to ear. She was rocking her head from side to side, patting her hands together, as I had seen the Negroes back home do when they began to get religion. I stepped back from Lally, forgetting all about him, wondering what was happening to Mrs. Smithers. Then I saw something was happening to Lally too. He was grinning, staring straight ahead at her, like a man in a trance. Suddenly he jumped on the davenport beside her, sitting on his heels, and began slapping her in the face furiously.

'Let me alone, let me alone,' he yelled, although I hadn't moved. 'I know what I'm doing. I know what I'm doing.'

I stood there looking, not moving a muscle. I didn't know what was happening, but I knew Lally wasn't mad any more and neither was she – and that whatever it was that was happening was strange and powerful and that I had never seen it happen to anybody before, and all at once I didn't mind, didn't care.

When he stopped slapping her she let the air out of her lungs and you could hear the exhalation all over the room. Her head rolled back and Lally leaned over and kissed her twice on the lips, and then he looked at me, blinking his eyes rapidly, trying to focus them, as if he were just now aware that somebody else was present. Then he looked back at Mrs. Smithers, who was holding her head up. Her face was as red as a beet, so red it seemed she had on no make-up at all.

I felt exhausted. I sat down in a chair. My legs were aching.

Without a word Mrs. Smithers stood up, reaching for her

trench coat and hat. Lally helped her into the coat. Neither
spoke to me, or even looked at me. They acted as if they
were alone at the end of the world. They walked to the door,
opened it, and went out, still not saying anything, leaving
the door open.

The rain blew in on the carpet and a gust of wind piled
through the room.

...*chapter ten*

It got dark early that night, about five thirty. The rain was still falling and it was beginning to get cold. I switched on a couple of lights and waited for Mona a little while longer and then went over to the drug store to have dinner.

When I had finished eating, I played the marble machine three or four times and then came back to the bungalow. Mona was sitting in front of the gas stove looking at a newspaper, and the house was nice and warm.

'I've been reading about you,' she said. 'Did you see this?'

'What is it?'

'Here – read it.'

She handed me the paper, the Hollywood *Citizen News*, that was opened to the movie page, pointing with her finger to a column. It was 'film-flam' by Sidney Skolsky.

'Mrs. Smithers's new leading man at the night spots is a handsome Georgian named Ralph Carston, which means you soon will be seeing him at your local theater. . . .'

'How'd he get my name?' I asked, surprised.

'What difference does it make? All that matters is he got it.'

'But I didn't meet him. I saw him, but I didn't meet him. Do you suppose he got my name from her?'

'I don't know how Skolsky works, but I suppose he has ways to find out those things. He, too, seems convinced that one way to get in the movies is to have a few dates with Smithers. . . . Did you have dinner?'

'Yes. Did you?'

'Yes.'

'You shouldn't have gone out in the rain.'

'Why not?'

'You'll catch your death of cold.'

'It's never bothered Garbo and I'm as durable as she is. . . . What's the matter with your hand?'

'Nothing.'

'Isn't that iodine on it?'

'Yes.'

'What's that doing on there?'

'I accidentally hit it on the stove.'

'I can see the swelling from here. You must have accidentally hit it pretty hard.'

'I did.'

We were quiet for a moment.

'Ralph – you didn't hit that woman?'

'I told you how it happened.'

'I don't believe you. Did you hit her?'

'No.'

'Honestly?'

'Honestly.'

'I believe that part of it, but I still don't believe you hit it on the stove. You don't want to tell me?'

'No.'

'All right. Only I can't imagine you in a fight.'

'Oh, I can take care of myself,' I said.

'I know you can. I didn't mean that. I meant you were so quiet and gentle I couldn't imagine you getting mad enough to fight anybody. I wouldn't want to see you get into trouble.'

'I'm not going to get into trouble,' I said.

'I hope not.'

'I'm not.'

I walked over to the window. It was good and black outside now. It was not raining so hard, it was more of a heavy mist.

'Would you like to go to a movie?' I asked her.

She shook her head.

'You go. I've got a date.'

'Well – ' I said slowly, 'I guess I can't blame you a hell of a lot.'

...chapter eleven

I did not hear any more from Mrs. Smithers for a couple of weeks. I tried to call her several times, but the operator said the phone had been disconnected. One day a card came from her from Ensenada, Mexico. It said:

'The rest has been wonderful. See you soon, dear boy. Love, E.S.'

I showed the card to Mona. 'I've been wondering where she was. It's been so quiet and peaceful around here lately,' she said. 'You never have told me why she left so suddenly.'

'I don't know myself.'

'It's mighty funny. Hot as she was for you and then for no reason at all she goes to Mexico. Mighty funny.'

'She's a funny woman.'

'Well – at least she's queer. That's a better word don't you think?'

I didn't say anything until I had finished sweeping the living-room and kitchen, opening all the windows and doors. It was a beautiful, warm day, like spring, the kind of day that makes you wonder why everybody in the world doesn't live in southern California.

Mona was using the telephone, calling some independent studios to try to get work.

'She could have pulled us out of this hole, all right,' I said. 'If she were here I wouldn't hesitate to ask her to lend us some money. Believe me, I've gotten over all that. Believe me, I have.'

I was glad now I had kept that hundred dollars Mrs. Smithers had given me the first day she came to the bungalow, but it made cold chills run up and down my spine to think how close I had come to giving it back. That money was all gone now; Mona had raised fifty dollars on her car from a refinancing company and most of that was gone. Money was our chief worry now. We still had two weeks to go before the rent was due again and our credit was good a little longer with Abie at the market, but the deadline was close enough to keep us thinking about it.

'Maybe I ought to try to get a job again,' I said.

'That's just a waste of time,' she said. 'Jobs are few and far between.'

'I wouldn't feel like as much of a heel if I tried,' I said.

'I don't see why you say that. You raised the last money – that's what we're living on now. You've done your part. We'll get a break soon.'

'I hope so,' I said, wishing Mrs. Smithers were back.

I felt lonely and depressed. I went upstairs to the bathroom and locked myself in and sat down on the toilet and had a good cry.

...part
two

...*chapter one*

The next afternoon Mona came in very excited.

'Guess what – I've got a job. A regular job.'

I got excited too.

'Doing what?'

'Let me get my breath,' she said, sitting down, fanning herself. 'I was coming by Magnin's a while ago and who should I bump into but Laura Eubanks.'

'Laura Eubanks?'

'I recognized her instantly, but I didn't want to speak to her first. You never can tell in Hollywood, you know.'

'Did she recognize you?'

'Recognize me? You'd thought I was her long-lost sister. Well, she insisted we go over to the Knickerbocker and have a drink. She said she'd enjoyed our talk that night at Mrs. Smithers's and had often wondered what'd become of me and was very much interested in me and what I was doing.'

'She could have found you if she'd been that interested,' I said. 'She could have asked Mrs. Smithers.'

'That's the usual routine – but let me finish. Her stand-in's just landed a stock contract at First National and she asked me to take the job. Thirty-five a week.'

Something hit me a jolt in the stomach and knocked all the excitement out of me.

'Is that the job? Stand-in?'

'Yes, of course.'

'You're a sucker to take it,' I said.

'Are you nuts? I'll get a regular salary, every week.'

'That's just it,' I said. 'What chance do you think you'll have in pictures taking a job as stand-in? They never get anywhere.'

'Her last one did. I just told you she landed a contract.'

'One in a thousand. One in twenty thousand.'

Mona looked at me, frowning.

'That's a peculiar attitude for you to take.'

'I've been here long enough to know a few things and that's one of them,' I said. 'You take that job and you can kiss your career good-bye.'

She got up and stood staring at me. All the excitement was gone out of her now.

'You overlook one thing, Mr. Carston,' she said in a flat voice. 'We've got to eat.'

She went to work that night, leaving me alone for the first time since I had known her. I wrote a letter home, not thinking about what I was writing, doing it mechanically and with great effort. The room was quiet and empty. When I had finished writing the letter, I called Mrs. Smithers's number and the operator cut in again, saying it was disconnected. I called information and asked for the new number, but she said there was none listed and I knew from this that Mrs. Smithers was still out of town. I tried a couple of stations on the radio, but that was no good either. I thought about going to see a movie, and then decided I didn't want to see a picture, that it would only make me feel worse to see people on the screen doing something I myself wanted to do.

I heard a noise at the kitchen door and went back and unlocked it.

'Jesus Christ!' I exclaimed.

It was Dorothy. She had on a man's shirt and trousers and an old pair of shoes.

'What the hell – ' I said, closing the door. 'Where'd you come from?'

'I escaped,' she said. 'Can you fix me something to eat?'

I fried her some eggs and fixed some coffee. She said she'd escaped from prison two days ago and would have been here sooner but she had to stick to the side roads where there was no traffic. She'd damn near died getting out of the desert, she said. In Bakersfield she'd stolen a Ford and that's how she got here.

She was very calm and showed no signs of travel. Except for the clothes she had on, it was the same old Dorothy.

'How's Mona?'

I told her about the job as stand-in for Laura Eubanks. She thought that was fine.

'Anything happened to you yet?'

'No – not yet.'

'It will,' she said. 'Just keep on pitching. How about another cup of coffee?'

I gave it to her.

'How'd you manage to escape?' I asked.

She smiled.

'It's a long story – '

'What are you going to do now?'

'Keep on going.'

'Where?'

'I don't know.'

'I wish you could stay here,' I said, 'but they'd find you sure. Aren't you afraid they'll find you?'

She shook her head.

'I don't suppose they look for women convicts as hard as they do men,' she said. 'Anyway, every day I'm out is that much velvet.'

'You're certainly not going to try to go back home to Ohio?'

Her face got a little sad.

'No – I'd be safer here than I would there. No, I guess I won't ever go home again.'

She drank the rest of her coffee.

'Can you let me have some money?' she said. 'I don't know that I'll ever pay you back, but I'll try.'

'I'm sorry, but I haven't got any. We're pretty hard up ourselves. I've got about sixty cents – '

'That wouldn't do any good,' she said.

I suddenly thought of something.

'You wait right here,' I said.

I went out the back way to the market.

'Hello, there, Barrymore,' Abie said, smiling.

You won't think it's funny when you find out what I want, I thought.

'I need twenty dollars in a hurry,' I said.

He looked shocked.

'Got a date, hunh? Got hot pants for some little Hollywood blonde, hunh?'

'On the level,' I said.

'Such a nice boy,' he said, pretending to be shocked. 'What for you want twenty dollars? To give to some clip joint?'

'Abe, this is a terrible emergency.'

He shrugged.

'To you it's an emergency, to me it's another touch. In Hollywood you can buy all you want for a dollar a throw. Who is it for twenty dollars? A king's mistress?'

I was getting impatient.

'Listen, Abe. You know I don't play around that way. I'll give you the money back tomorrow when Mona comes home. I'd get it from her, but she isn't here. I'll give it back to you or I'll work it out in the market – but I've got to have it. Please!'

He looked at me for a moment and then shrugged again and opened the cash register.

'Me, I'm a pushover – ' he said, counting out the money. 'Of all the places for me to go in business I pick this bummers' town. In any other place by now I'm rich as Guggenheim.'

He handed me the money. I could have kissed him.

'Thank you, Abe.'

'It ain't thanks I want, it's my dough back.'

'Thank you.'

'Me, I'm a pushover,' he said, shaking his head.

You're a wonderful man, Abe Epstein, I thought, running across the parking lot, back to the apartment.

I gave Dorothy the money, and tears rolled down her cheeks.

'I don't know how to thank you.'

'Forget it.'

She started to say something, but could not because of her emotions.

'You'd better go, Dorothy,' I said. 'And if we can help you any more, drop us a line.'

She nodded, wiping her eyes.

'I'm sorry Mona isn't here,' she said. 'Can I write her a note?'

'Sure,' I said, leading her in to the desk.

She scribbled a note and handed it to me. I followed her back into the kitchen. She picked up a paper bag, saying: 'I fixed me a couple of sandwiches. I didn't know about the money then.'

'That's all right,' I said. 'I'll go out to the street with you. Where'd you park your car?'

'In front.'

'If I were you I'd take a bus or something,' I said as we went out the back way. 'It's bad enough you being an escaped prisoner, but riding in a stolen car makes it twice as bad.'

'I'll fix that,' she said. 'I'll get some other licenses.'

She stopped by the car, leaned over, and kissed me good-bye.

At that moment a cop grabbed her. I was paralyzed with surprise. Before I could move or say anything, before I could even think, a second cop grabbed me.

'Just a minute,' he said. 'What is this?'

Neither Dorothy nor I spoke.

'Whose car is this?' asked the first one.

'Mine,' Dorothy said.

'Who is this guy – your partner?'

Then my brain stopped spinning and was very clear. All of a sudden I realized that these policemen were only after the stolen car and that they had not recognized Dorothy, had no idea she was an escaped convict.

'That car's mine,' I said. 'This girl's just a friend of mine. I stole the car. She doesn't know anything about it.'

I knew that if I could get them to let Dorothy go I could soon prove I hadn't stolen the car. I'd never been to Bakersfield in my life.

'He didn't steal it,' Dorothy said. 'I stole it. He's the one who doesn't know anything about it.'

I tried to catch her eye to shut her up, to try to signal to her what I was doing, but she paid no attention.

'She's crazy,' I said. 'I stole that car in Bakersfield this afternoon.'

The cops looked at each other.

'Who's got the key?' asked the first one.

'I have,' Dorothy said, taking it out of her pocket.

'That doesn't prove a thing,' I said.

Five or six people had gathered around.

'All right, Alphonse and Gaston,' the second cop said, 'we'll take a ride to headquarters.'

They started marching us away.

'Wait a minute,' I said. 'I've got to get my coat. I've got to close the house. I left the back door open.'

'You let us worry about the door, son,' he said, leading

us to their car. They put me in front and Dorothy in the back. I wanted to tip her off to shut up and let me take the blame so she should get away, but I had no chance.

We were both booked on suspicion of grand larceny and locked in different cells.

I did not sleep any that night.

...*chapter two*

In the morning I was notified that an additional charge had been placed against me – assisting an escape. The note Dorothy had written Mona, to tell her good-bye, in which she said I was swell to let her have the twenty dollars, had become very damaging when the police discovered who Dorothy really was.

About ten o'clock Mona came to see me with a lawyer named Holbrook. I told him how it had all happened, and he seemed very pessimistic.

'We haven't got a leg to stand on,' he said. 'We can prove you had nothing to do with stealing the car, but the other is serious. I don't want to give you any false hopes, I want you to know exactly what we're up against. It looks bad.'

'But I wasn't trying to break the law,' I said. 'I only gave her the money so she could.'

'I know, I know,' Holbrook said. 'You acted on pure impulse. But you did give her the money, and when the police arrested you, you told them you had stolen the car and that she had nothing to do with it.'

'You see why I did that, don't you?'

He smiled.

'So do the police – now. You were trying to help her get

away. That burst of heroism you had isn't going to help us any.' He turned to Mona. 'You understand, don't you?'

'Yes,' she said.

'But what about getting me out of here?' I asked.

'We can't do anything about that now.'

'But, my God,' I said, 'I don't want to stay in jail.'

'The only thing I can do,' Holbrook said, 'is to try to have the examining trial as soon as I can. When they set your bond we can get you out. You know anybody to go your bond?'

I shook my head.

'Do you?' he asked Mona.

'How much will it be?'

'I don't know. Not more than twenty-five hundred dollars, I should think.'

'I might be able to think of somebody,' she said. 'Whose court will this come up in when they do have the trial? I mean what judge's?'

'Oh, let's not worry about that yet.'

'I want to know,' Mona said.

'I can't tell yet,' Holbrook said. 'We'll have to wait until they assign it. May be any one of half a dozen courts. Why?'

'Well – ' she said slowly, 'suppose this case went to a judge who was a little more inclined to look at the human side of it than the legal side?'

The lawyer shook his head skeptically.

'That'd be fine – if we could finagle the case into this court.'

'We'll finagle,' Mona said. She took a five-dollar bill out of her purse and handed it to me. 'Here – you'll need this.'

'For what?' I asked.

Holbrook reached over and took the bill out of my hands.

'Have you five ones?' he asked Mona.

'What's the difference?'

He smiled.

'A lot. Just to be on the safe side – '

Mona looked through her purse and found three ones and some change. She gave me that.

'When you buy something spend a dollar at a time,' Holbrook said. He gave Mona back the five and looked at me. 'Keep your chin up now and trust us. We'll get you out of here as quickly as we can.'

'Is there anything you want?' Mona asked.

'No.'

'I'll come to see you tomorrow.'

'What about your job?'

'I'll take care of that,' she said, patting my arm, walking away with the lawyer.

I watched them until they turned the corner of the corridor, out of sight. Then I walked across the cell to the window. The jail was in the Hall of Justice and I was on the twelfth floor. From my window I could see part of downtown Los Angeles, the wholesale district and the railroad tracks and box cars. You know what I was wishing when I saw the box cars. . . .

I could not see any part of Hollywood. That was in the opposite direction, behind me.

...chapter three

It was summertime in Georgia. Butch Siegfried and I were lying on our backs on the bank of Crow Creek. We had just been swimming in the deep hole where the biggest catfish lived, and now we were lying in the grass in the shade of the elm tree.

'Ralph – '

'What?'

'What're you gonna be when you grow up?'

'I dunno. Sailor. What're you?'

'I dunno.'

'What'd you ask for, then?'

'I dunno.'

It was nice here, like this. Through the branches and leaves of the elm tree you could see the pale blue of the sky and an occasional white cloud that drifted by. The only noises were of birds singing and insects rattling their wings and legs.

'Ralph – how far is New York?'

'I dunno. – What're you asking all these questions for? Shut up and be quiet.'

'I was just thinking – '

'Thinking what?'

'About New York.'

'What about New York?'

'Nothing. Just how much I'd like to go there.'

'You will when you grow up. Your father'll take you.'

'I don't want to go like that.'

I rolled over and looked at him, putting my head in my hand.

'You must be loony. That's getting there, isn't it?'

'But if I go with my father I'll have to come back. I want to stay. I don't want to work in the store.'

'You don't? With all the candy and roller skates and bicycles and fishing stuff? You must be loony.'

'I wanna be like you. You do whatever you please. Every time I come swimming or fishing I have to sneak off.'

Suddenly, standing above us was the enormous form of Mr. Siegfried.

'You get up from there this minute and put your clothes on,' he said to Butch. 'I try to teach you the business and you loaf all the time.'

I scrambled up and dived into the creek, afraid he would whip me too.

'You stop teaching my boy how to loaf,' he yelled at me.

I dived under the water, and when I came up I bumped my head on something, seeing a million stars. I thought it was the root of the elm tree and I reached up to grab it and saw it was the steel bunk above me.

'Here he is,' the jailer was saying.

I looked around and there was Mrs. Smithers.

'Hello, dear boy,' she said, sticking her hand through the bars.

I sat on the bunk a moment or two until I could get my bearings, and then I went over and shook hands with her.

'You dear, dear boy,' she said. 'I got here as fast as I could. I just read about it in the paper.'

'Thank you, ma'am,' I said. 'You certainly are nice to come to see me.'

'Why, of course I'm not. A most peculiar thing happened. All day yesterday at Coronado I had a feeling that something was wrong. I didn't know what it was or whom it concerned – it was simply a premonition. And this is what it was.'

'I didn't do anything,' I said. 'Not really.'

'It doesn't make any difference whether you did or not,' she said. 'I'll have you out of here in no time. I've already seen a friend of mine – a political friend, you know – and he has promised me faithfully that you'll be out tomorrow.'

I didn't know whether to believe her, but I finally did because I wanted to. When you are in jail as I was, you grab at the least little ray of hope as long as it is not absolutely impossible.

'Thank you, Mrs. Smithers,' I said, feeling the tears coming into my eyes. 'Thank you, very much.'

'Jailer – jailer,' she called.

A couple of prisoners across the corridor started razzing Mrs. Smithers.

'Goddam, what a dish that is!'

'Lookit the rocks on that baby!'

'Hey, buddy – are you the Prince of Wales?'

'Boy, what a keister she's packing around.'

Mrs. Smithers was trying not to pay any attention to these remarks, but I could see she was getting nervous.

'I'd like to be over there with you birds for just a couple of minutes,' I yelled at them.

They screamed back and the jailer came up.

'Nix, you guys,' he said.

They shut up.

'Lady,' he said, 'maybe you better go.'

'I'm going,' she said. 'Jailer, this young man is a special friend of mine and I want him to have all the comfort you can give him,' she went on, feeling around in her purse. She folded a bill in her hand and held it out.

'We'll do all we can for him, lady,' the jailer said, paying no attention to the hand that held the bill.

Mrs. Smithers kept poking at him with her hand, trying to get him to take the money.

'Thanks, lady, just the same,' he said. 'I don't want your money.'

Mrs. Smithers seemed disappointed. She returned the bill to her purse.

'Good-bye, dear boy,' she said. 'Tomorrow we'll have have lunch together.'

'Thank you, Mrs. Smithers. I hope so. I hope your friend means what he says.'

'Oh, he does. Good-bye.'

'Good-bye.'

She went off with the jailer, waving her hand at me.

The two prisoners across the corridor waited until the jailer and Mrs. Smithers were out of sight and then started in again.

'Good-bye, dear boy.'

'What are you son – a faggot?'

'Whoops, my dear! Tomorrow we'll have lunch together.'

'In a pig's eye you'll have lunch tomorrow.'

The jailer came back, walking very fast.

'Pipe down, boys,' he said quietly.

'Put me in there with those bastards,' I said. 'I'll pipe 'em down.'

'You pipe down too,' the jailer said.

I went over and crawled into the bunk again. I wanted to go to sleep and not wake up until tomorrow; when I waked up I wanted it to be outside somewhere. I closed my eyes, trying to go to sleep, trying to pick up the dream where I had left off when I was swimming, before I hit my head. . . .

That night the jailer brought me a box of candy that Mona had left, showing me the note she had scribbled on the bottom of the box.

'R. Sorry I couldn't see you, but it was after visiting hours. Don't worry. We are doing all we can. M.'

Inside the box on top of the candy was a letter from home. It was just the same as all the other letters Mother wrote me, saying that everything back there was the same and that they were glad I was getting along so well.

...chapter four

The preliminary trial was held the next day. Mona, Mrs. Smithers, and Holbrook, the lawyer, were there. Holbrook told me to plead guilty to the charge of assisting an escape so we could expedite the matter of a bond. The other charge had been dismissed.

The judge called the two policemen who had arrested Dorothy and me in front of the bungalow court and they told how it happened that they had spotted the stolen car parked in Vine Street and had waited until Dorothy and I had come out to get in it. They admitted that at that time they did not know Dorothy was an escaped convict. A matron told of finding twenty dollars in Dorothy's pocket, and another policeman, the one who had searched me, told about the letter he had found in my pocket that Dorothy had written to Mona telling her about the money I had given her.

I leaned over and told Holbrook that all this was true, and that I had admitted it, and asked him why the judge didn't hurry up and get it over with.

'This is a formality,' he said. 'This is for the record – for later.'

There was not much else said. The judge declared that the

evidence warranted holding me for trial in the superior-court division and fixed my bail at three thousand dollars.

Mrs. Smithers stepped forward and said she was there to furnish bond, and Holbrook, Mrs. Smithers, and the prosecuting attorney went into the judge's chambers. I asked one of the policemen if that meant I was free.

'You will be in a minute if the bond's any good,' he said.

'She's good for a thousand times that,' I said.

Mona was staring out the window, her face pensive. When she felt me looking at her, she turned around.

'It's funny how our lives are mixed up with this court-house,' she said in a low voice. 'It shouldn't be. All we want is to be left alone.'

'One of these days – ' I began.

'I hope so,' she said. 'I had a session with Judge Boggess yesterday afternoon.'

'You did? What'd he say?'

'He's going to ask for the case in his court. So now all we have to do is pray for him to be re-elected so he will be back on the bench when the trial comes off.'

'That's fine, but I hope you didn't say anything to him you shouldn't have said.'

'Oh,' she said, smiling. 'I didn't. It was all very ethical.'

I knew by the look in her eye what she meant.

Mrs. Smithers came back into the room, beaming, her arms outstretched, followed by Holbrook.

'Come, dear boy – you're free,' she said.

I looked at Holbrook.

'That's right,' he said, 'thanks to Mrs. Smithers's generosity. She's been a friend in need, all right.'

'Thank you, Mrs. Smithers,' I said. 'Thank you, too,' I said to Holbrook.

'Forget it,' he said. 'Now, there's just one thing. You must not leave town or change your address without notifying the court – or me. Under no circumstances must you do that.'

'I won't,' I said. 'When do I have to come back?'

'I can't say exactly – the case will be set for sometime next month, perhaps – or the month after. But don't worry. We're coming up before a very fair and impartial judge – Judge Boggess. A good friend of mine, incidentally. I thought it best that Judge Boggess – '

'That was swell of you,' Mona said. 'You were very thoughtful to get Judge Boggess to ask for this case. Yes, sir, you were thoughtful as all hell.'

Holbrook frowned, not quite understanding the sarcasm in Mona's tone? He didn't know she was the one who had got Judge Boggess to ask for the case. In a moment he made a movement to go.

'Well – ' he said. 'Mrs. Smithers, on behalf of my client I want to thank you again. Good-bye, Miss Matthews. I'll keep in touch with you, Ralph.'

He walked out.

'Come, come, you two,' Mrs. Smithers said, putting her arms around us, walking out with us.

Walter, the chauffeur, was waiting at the steps. He saluted and went down the street to get the car.

'Where shall we have lunch?' she asked.

'I've got to get back to the studio,' Mona said. 'They're waiting for me.'

'My, my!' Mrs. Smithers said. 'That's too bad. Can't we drop you there? What studio is it?'

'Thanks – I've got my car,' Mona said. 'Good-bye, Mrs. Smithers. See you later, Ralph.'

'Sure,' I said, watching her cross the street.

'Where shall we have lunch, dear boy? I told you we'd have lunch together today. Where shall we go?'

'I'm not very hungry,' I said. 'I had a lot of candy this morning. Besides, I'd like to take a bath.'

Mrs. Smithers smiled.

'How charming!' she said. 'How charming!'

Walter brought the car in front of the steps and we got in.

'Would you like to bathe at my place – or yours?'

'Mine,' I said. 'My clothes are there.'

We started off through the traffic. I relaxed in the car, looking out the window, looking up at the Hall of Justice, where I had been a prisoner. It was the first time I had got a good look at the building. I'm glad to be out of that place, I thought. There's nothing like freedom.

Mrs. Smithers put her hand on my leg and started talking. . . .

We had dinner that night alone in an enormous room lighted only by candles. She sat at one end of the table and I sat at the other, but I could hardly see her for the flowers and the candelabra. There were two butlers. I had never seen such elegance. It was like a scene from a movie. Every room in her house and everything about the house seemed like a scene from a movie.

We had just started eating when she said:

'I can't see you, dear boy.'

'I can't see you either,' I said.

When the butlers came to take the soup cups she told them to move my chair down by her, on the side. I stood up while they changed it.

'Isn't that better?' she asked, patting my hand.

'Yes, ma'am,' I said, trying to hide my embarrassment. I was not so much embarrassed by her as I was wondering what the butlers would think about my manners. I had never been to a house where they had butlers before, where they passed silver platters for you to help yourself, but I tried to imitate her, hoping I made no mistakes.

'Like this, Ralph,' she said, holding up her knife and fork, showing me how to use them. 'By the tips. Hold them lightly. Don't saw your meat – and don't stab at it.'

I was glad for the candles, so the butlers wouldn't see me blush.

'I'm sorry,' I said.

She smiled.

'You are charming,' she said. 'Don't be self-conscious now. You are no stranger here – this is your home.'

'Yes, ma'am,' I said.

All through the dinner she watched me like a hawk, showing me how to eat and how to handle my glass and how to use my napkin. By the time it was over I was not embarrassed any more. I was beginning to enjoy it. I knew that when I got to be a movie star these were the things I would have to know.

A few more lessons like this, I thought, and I'll be ready for any kind of a test they want to give me.

That dinner made me realize, for the first time, that there was a big difference in the way people lived. I had seen dinners like this in the movies, but I had never paid much attention because they were movies. This was different. . . .

She had coffee and brandy in the living-room and she poured Cointreau for me. It was sweet and pleasant. She taught me how to drink this too. She was patient and quiet and very nice. I couldn't believe that this was the same woman who had been so wild that afternoon in Mona's bungalow, that time with Lally.

'Where's Lally?' I asked.

'I was saving that for a surprise,' she said. 'He's gone east. To New York.'

'New York?' I asked.

'He wanted to go into a show. He had an offer – a good offer – and so he went. He left by plane this morning.'

I did not say anything. I did not know then that she had thrown him out to make room for me.

'You don't care about going out tonight, do you? You don't like the night places, do you?'

'It's much nicer here,' I said.

'Would you like to see some movies?'

'I don't like movies much either.'

'Silly. I mean here. We'll show them here.'

'Can you show movies here?' I asked, surprised.

'These movies we can,' she said.

'I'd like that,' I said. 'But I'd better call Mona. I'll have to tell her I'll be late.'

She laughed.

'You weren't planning on going back there tonight, were you?'

'Why – yes.'

'No,' she said, putting down the coffee cup. 'Tomorrow you can go and get your things, but not tonight. You wouldn't have me stay in this big house all alone, would you?'

I didn't know what to say. All along I had known something like this was coming and now that it had I didn't know what to say. I didn't want to offend her, because she had been so nice to me. 'Why can't she always be like she was a minute ago?' I asked myself.

'Telephone Mona,' she said. 'Tell her you're staying here.'

'Yes, ma'am,' I replied.

She got up.

'And then we'll have the movies. Come, I'll show you the phone – in that powder room. When you finish, come upstairs.'

'Yes, ma'am,' I said. I closed the door and dialled Mona's number.

'Hello – Mona?'

'Yes.'

'This is Ralph. How are you?'

'All right. A little tired. Where are you?'

'At Mrs. Smithers.'

'I see. I've been waiting for you to have dinner.'

'Well – '

'When are you coming?'

'Look, Mona – I'm in kind of a spot.'

'Oh.'

'I may be late.'

There was a pause. Then:

'All right, Ralph.'

'I hope you're not sore, Mona.'

'Of course not. I understand.'

'Why don't you go to a movie or something?'

'Oh, don't worry about me. Ralph – '

'Yes.'

'Do be careful.'

'I will, Mona. If I don't see you tonight I'll see you tomorrow.'

Another pause.

'All right. You were sweet to call.'

'Aw, of course I wasn't. If I don't see you tonight I'll see you tomorrow.'

'All right, Ralph. I'm off tomorrow. Eubanks is sick and they're shooting around her. I'm going down to see Dorothy. I do wish you'd go with me.'

'Sure, I'll go. Sure I will.'

'All right, Ralph.'

'Good-bye, Mona.'

'Good-bye.'

I hung up the phone and stood there, looking in the mirror of the dressing-table. I couldn't put off looking at myself any longer.

'I couldn't help it, could I?' I said to the image in the glass.

'Don't speak to me,' the image replied.

'You know I don't want to stay here, but what can I do? If she hadn't gone my bond where would I be?'

'Still in jail – but you'd been better off – '

'Why do you talk like that? You don't seem to realize that, after all, I'm a lucky fellow.'

'Lucky! How?'

'Because she takes an interest in me. You know what a tough town this is. Why, there are ten thousand fellows in Hollywood right now who'd give their arms to trade places with me. With Mrs. Smithers sponsoring me I can't miss.'

'She hasn't done you any good so far.'

'That's where you're wrong. Look at tonight. I took my first lesson in how to be a gentleman.'

'You're going to get some more too. Wait till she gets you upstairs.'

'What's going to happen then?'

'You know.'

'No, I don't.'

'Well, something will, you can bet on that.'

'I don't care. I'm going to be in the movies before I get through and I don't care how I get there. I've got more chance here than I have sitting home waiting for the phone to ring. There're ten thousand fellows in Hollywood who'd like to be in my shoes.'

'That's what you think.'

'Ralph, Ralph!' Mrs. Smithers called.

I looked at the image out of the corner of my eye.

'That's right,' it said. 'Don't look at me.'

I snapped off the light, went out of the powder room, went slowly upstairs.

Mrs. Smithers was waiting for me in the bedroom. She had changed into a cream-colored négligé, and there was a square box in the middle of the floor, looking like a salesman's sample case. She bent over and opened it. It was a small projection machine.

'Take this out,' she said.

I lifted the machine out while she moved down by the bed and unfolded a tripod screen.

'Put the projector on that table,' she said.

In a minute she came back and plugged in the cable.

'Watch me,' she said. 'You must learn how to work this.'

She took a small roll of film out of a can and began threading it into the machine.

'This isn't a talking picture, is it?' I asked.

'No – sixteen millimetre,' she said. 'See how I do this. Catch it on the sprockets and loop it like this.'

'Who's in this picture?'

'Don't be curious, and watch me.'

'I am watching you,' I said. There were about twenty or twenty-five cans of film on the davenport.

'There,' she said. 'Now turn out the light.'

I turned out the light.

'Now come sit by me.'

I sat down beside her on the davenport.

'I don't want you to be frightened at this,' she said. 'Remember it's just a moving picture.'

'I won't be.'

She snapped off the pilot light on the projector and started the picture. *Their Night Out*, the title said.

Two men were sitting at a table playing cards. There was

a knock at the door. One of them got up and opened it, admitting two girls. They didn't kiss or shake hands or anything else, they all started taking off their clothes. One of them literally tore his shirt off.

'They don't waste any time, do they?' I said, just to have something to say, to try to cover my self-consciousness.

'That's to save footage,' Mrs. Smithers said. 'Haven't you ever seen pictures like this before?'

'No, ma'am,' I said, and this was the truth.

'Well,' she said, 'you know, Ralph – for a grown man you've seen very little of life.'

'Yes, ma'am.'

'How charming! Look at what they're doing now.'

I looked – and I was thankful the room was dark so she couldn't see my face. . . .

...*chapter five*

The next morning I returned to the bungalow court. Johnny Hill, the drunk Mona had put to bed one night, was there. Mona greeted me casually, as if I had only stepped out for a few minutes. I realized she was trying not to make me feel uncomfortable. She knew as well as I did what had happened last night. I could tell that by the look in her face.

'How's the novel?' I asked Hill.

'What novel?'

'The one you were going to do about Hollywood extras.'

He suddenly remembered.

'Oh, that. I've postponed it until spring. I'm back in the publicity game.'

'At Excelsior,' Mona said.

'Excelsior? Do you know Jonathan Balter?'

'Never heard of him. What does he do?'

'He's the man who brought me out here. He's a talent scout.'

'In that case, I have no desire to know him. I have a sufficiently large acquaintance among the racketeers now.' He nodded significantly at Mona. 'And you better think it over, babe.'

Mona laughed.

'He's warning me,' she said.

'You got any influence with this twist, Carston?' he asked me. 'If you have, you better use it to talk some sense into her head.'

'What about Cagney and Montgomery and Crawford and Tone?' Mona said. 'They're doing it.'

'They're stars,' he said. 'There's a slight difference between their position and yours.' He looked at me. 'You better make her stop it while the stopping's good.'

'Stop what?'

'All this organizing.'

'What organizing?'

'What organizing?' he repeated, exasperated. 'Where've you been?'

'I don't know what you're talking about,' I said.

'The actors are all going on strike,' he said. 'They're going on a strike because they want to improve the conditions of the extras. All the big stars are going to walk out. Mona's been doing a lot of talking on the set.'

'I'll keep on talking too,' she said.

'That's what I'm afraid of. You're standing in for Eubanks. She's an Excelsior star – and a big one. Every chance you get you're talking to the people on the set about organizing. Excelsior doesn't like that. Excelsior'll kick you out on your can if you don't stop.'

'See?' Mona said to me. 'He's threatening me. He's trying to intimidate me.'

'Christ, will you be serious?' he said. 'Excelsior hasn't sent me here to warn you. But I work there and I know their sentiment and you're a friend of mine and I'm just telling

123

you. You've been here long enough to know that anybody who opens his mouth about organizing anything is classified as a radical and black-balled pronto. I went through that last scrape with the Writers' Guild. I sat in the producers' meetings and heard them tell the writers what to do.'

'That's a violation of some law or other,' Mona said. 'They can't do that.'

'These babies can do any goddam thing they want to,' he said. 'They can coerce and browbeat and violate all the laws they want to. What the hell, they make the laws. They make the laws and they own the courts – didn't they elect a governor by the simple and subtle expedient of so-called news reels? Don't you remember what they did to Upton Sinclair? Were you here then?'

'No,' I said.

'Well, no matter,' he said. 'It's a black chapter in California politics – as black as the Tom Mooney frame-up. So don't tell me they can't do things. You can do anything you want in this country if you're big enough – and if you don't think so, take a gander at the great national panorama someday.' He looked at Mona. 'And you'd better be a good girl too.'

Mona didn't say anything for a moment. Hill got up to go.

'Don't get me wrong,' he said. 'I think it's a swell idea, but the time isn't ripe yet. I'm telling you as a pal to lay off. I've been here a long time and I've seen too many things happen.'

'Thanks, Johnny,' Mona said.

'In one ear and out the other,' he said. 'Well – I'll be seeing you.'

He went out.

'What is all this?' I asked.

'Nothing – nothing,' she said. 'I'll get my hat.'

'Do you suppose they'll let us see Dorothy?'

'Certainly – they did yesterday.'

She adjusted her hat and I helped her into the coat to her suit.

'I've got a car in front,' I said.

She shook her head.

'Let's go in mine,' she said. 'For old times' sake.'

'All right,' I said. 'For old times' sake.' . . .

On our way downtown we talked of trivial things, of anything that came into our minds, as people do to keep a conversation alive, fearful that if it dies or even lags for a moment, the other person will ask a question or say something you don't want to hear: about how silly and pointless we thought the Chesterfield billboards were and whether or not we would (if we had money enough) buy the products whose ads appealed to us, about how much we liked the Skippy ads for gasoline and the one of the swimming-suit company where the boy and the girl were kissing under water; talking about people we saw on the street and the names of stores; and passing Angelus Temple, we started talking about Aimee, which kept us busy until we got into the traffic near the Hall of Justice. . . .

When we asked the jailer if we could see Dorothy Trotter he leaned back in his chair and said she wasn't there any more.

Mona and I looked at each other, thinking the same thing, that she had been taken back to prison.

'When did she leave?' Mona asked.

'Are you friends of hers?'

'Yes,' Mona and I said together.

'You'll find her over at the morgue,' the jailer said. 'She hanged herself early this morning.'

...*chapter*
six

Dorothy was lying on a table, her face very white. Around her neck, directly under her chin, was a black mark. She had hanged herself with one of her stockings, the man said, showing us that one leg was still bare.

Mona walked around the table looking at her. I followed directly behind. Neither of us said anything. I didn't even feel anything. That wasn't right, I knew. I should have felt something. But I didn't. There was no expression on Mona's face, either; no sign of emotion. Neither one of us believed what we saw. This couldn't be Dorothy. Not Dorothy. She never had worried about anything. She would be the last person in the world to kill herself. This couldn't be Dorothy, stretched out here on her back, dead.

But it was Dorothy. And she was dead.

'Well – ' Mona said quietly, looking at the white face, 'I guess that's one way out.'

'She's better off,' I said, keeping my voice down. 'She's better off than she's ever been.'

A couple of newspaper photographers came up and took flashlight pictures of the body.

We started out.

'Hey,' one of the photographers called to the officer who

worked there, 'got the stocking this girl hanged herself with?'

'No,' the officer said.

'That's too bad,' the photographer answered. 'Like to get a shot at that stocking. You know, the Instrument of Death.'

Mona and I stepped out into the street. She was looking around, preoccupied.

'Wait a minute,' she said.

I didn't know what was the matter with her. She disappeared into a drug store, and in a minute she came hurrying back across the street.

'Just a minute,' she said, going into the morgue again.

I followed her in. The two photographers were still there, standing beside Dorothy. They watched Mona approach, backing up a little. She had taken something from under her coat, I couldn't see what, and was arranging Dorothy's hands to hold it. I walked over to see what was happening.

'Take a picture of that,' she was saying.

'What's the matter with you?' one photographer said. 'Those are magazines.'

Now I saw what Mona had done, what she went across to the drug store for. She had brought three or four movie magazines and had propped up Dorothy's hands so that she appeared to be holding them in death.

The morgue officer came up.

'What's going on here?' he asked.

'Nothing,' Mona said. 'Only these gentlemen wanted a picture of the Instrument of Death – and I've given them several instruments. Go ahead and shoot those,' she said to the photographers. They were staring at her as if she were crazy. 'That's what really killed her. Why don't you shoot that? Isn't it glamorous enough? Go ahead – show the world an authentic picture of Hollywood.'

'Outta here, you,' the officer said.

I put my arm around Mona, helping her outside to the street. She did not break down until we were in the car, coming home . . . .

I had a luncheon date with Mrs. Smithers for one thirty at the Beverly Brown Derby, but I didn't keep it. That old feeling of hating places like that and the people who went there was back with me. After I had driven Mona home and seen that she was comfortable, I got in the roadster Mrs. Smithers had let me use and drove to her house.

She came home around three o'clock. I was waiting in the patio.

'You shouldn't treat me like this,' she said, pouting, but I could feel the force behind her words, behind all that pretense of injury. 'I waited for you until a few minutes ago.'

'I didn't want lunch,' I said.

'Where'd you go? Were you with Mona?'

'Yes,' I said.

I explained where we had been – and what we had seen.

'How ghastly!' she exclaimed. 'You dear boy, what an awful thing to see! A dead girl.'

'It wasn't awful,' I said. 'Maybe she had the right idea, at that. Maybe she did.'

129

She came over and put her hands on my shoulder.

'You mustn't say that,' she said. 'I shouldn't have let you go away in the first place. Now you're morbid.'

'I'm not morbid,' I said.

'Yes, you are. I won't let you out of my sight again. You're too sensitive to things like that.'

'Mrs. Smithers,' I said, 'can I talk to you a minute?'

'Why, you dear boy,' she laughed, 'we are talking.'

'Seriously, I mean.'

'No, absolutely not,' she said. 'We must never be serious. Every time you get serious you disappoint me.'

I sat down facing the swimming-pool. She finally sat down beside me, taking off her hat.

'You should have been with me at luncheon,' she said. 'I want you to meet my friends. You'll like them. Several of them are going to San Simeon next week. Would you like to go to San Simeon?'

'No,' I said.

'Do you know where San Simeon is? Do you know what it is?'

'No.'

'It's Mr. Hearst's estate up the coast. You've surely heard of it.'

'I don't think so,' I said.

'How quaint!' she said, smiling. 'San Simeon is Mr. Hearst's castle on the seacoast. He has hundreds and hundreds of acres. He entertains only the dukes and duchesses and the important people.'

'I still don't want to go,' I said. 'I don't like Mister Hearst.'

'You mustn't say that. You don't even know him.'

'My father knows him. My father used to work on a newspaper.'

She seemed horrified.

'You must not say things like that,' she said sharply. 'Mr. Hearst is a very important and a very lovable man. You must not be a Bolsheviki.'

'Look, Mrs. Smithers,' I said, 'you've been swell to me. You went bail for me and everything and I owe you a lot. But I don't think I'm going to like living here so much.'

She leaned over close to me.

'We won't show those pictures again,' she said.

'It's not that.'

'You're not remorseful about the other, are you? It had to happen sometime, you know?'

'It's not that either.'

She straightened up, smiling in a relieved way.

'Well, then dear boy – give me a chance. I'm just starting. You've got your own car and you can have your own friends too. I'm not that selfish.'

'Mrs. Smithers, it's just that I don't feel I'm getting anywhere. I want to be in pictures. The way it is now I'm farther away from pictures than ever. I appreciate all you've done for me, the car and everything, but I want to be in pictures. I want to be a star. I want to be famous.'

She looked at me, frowning.

'It takes time,' she said. 'This is a perfect arrangement for you. I know all the picture people. I know all the people who can help you. I want to see you be a star too, Ralph. You know that, don't you? – Don't you?'

131

'I suppose so.'

She reached over and squeezed my hand.

'You're upset. Seeing that dead girl did this. Why don't you take a nap?'

'I feel all right,' I said.

'You'll be up late tonight. We've guests coming. You'd better nap with me.'

'I'm all right,' I said again.

She got up and kissed me on the forehead. As she was leaning over me, kissing me, the front of her dress sagged and I had to close my eyes to keep from seeing her breasts.

'You must have faith in me, dear boy. You must have faith and trust me.'

She walked away. The words that were in the back of my mind before she came were still there, unspoken. I hadn't said what I had wanted to. I looked at the swimming-pool, remembering the first time I had ever seen it, the night that girl, Fay Capeheart, was swimming in the nude. It had all seemed so wonderful then. I was full of optimism and confidence. I honestly believed it would be only a few days before I would succeed in pictures. I couldn't understand now, looking at the same scene, why it wasn't still wonderful. Something had happened, I didn't know what. All I knew was that I was miserable and missed Mona and that cheap little bungalow more than I had missed anything in my life – anything.

...chapter
seven

The dinner was tedious and long-drawn-out. There were twelve people in all, and Mrs. Smithers had put on two extra butlers to help serve. The guests were all picture executives and stars with three exceptions: myself, the writer who had jumped into the swimming-pool that first night with all his clothes on and who still was wearing a sweatshirt, and a girl of about twenty-two named Rose Otto. I liked her best of all. She had just finished as an attraction at one of the amusement piers where she had broken the world's record for being buried alive.

I could tell from the uncertain way she acted at the table that she was feeling the same way I had felt when I ate here the night before. But she needn't have. From the way this writer was eating, you would have thought the girl and I had come from the best families in the world.

Everybody was talking pictures. Two of the producers were very much concerned about the threatened strike of the stars and had no hesitancy in saying so. But the third producer, across the table, laughed at them.

'Three thousand dollars a week they make and they should go on strike?' he said. 'Don't be silly. Nobody strikes making that much money.'

'You can't laugh this off.'

'Strikes is right up my alley,' he said. He leaned across the table and waved a cigar. 'Look – strikes is never won without public opinion. All right. The stars walk out. And so we tell the newspapers: "We are dumbfounded. We are amazed. We are surprised. They are getting from two thousand to five thousand dollars a week and they are not satisfied. What kick have they got coming? Working conditions? A coal miner digs all day, maybe a little more, maybe a little less. Does he kick? Five thousand a week and they're beefing." So – the newspaper prints that. The public reads it. Pretty soon the public think the stars are crazy for striking. Strikes, phooey!'

Everybody at the table nodded except the two producers who had started the conversation.

'You're too pessimistic,' one of them said. 'We – '

'Psst! Psst! the writer said. 'Not pessimistic. Optimistic. *Op*-timistic.'

'All right,' the producer said. 'Optimistic. What I started to say was this: we can break any other strike in the world but actors'. Writers we can bring in for a hundred dollars a week and teach 'em the business, directors we can make – but not actors. Not stars. They've got us.'

'Phooey.'

'Gentlemen, gentlemen,' Mrs. Smithers said. She looked at the writer. 'Heinrich, can't you do something about those two? You tell us a story.'

Heinrich got up and bowed with great dignity.

'Dear lady,' he said, 'what you're asking me to do, in plain language, is give these gentlemen the bum's rush.'

Everybody laughed.

'But that is not a sagacious thing for me to do. One of them – that one – is my present employer. The other one is a potential employer.'

'Louder,' somebody said.

Heinrich nodded, stepping up in his chair, stepping from that to the table. He kicked a couple of dishes away with his foot. He was a little drunk.

'I will tell you an idea I have for a new picture,' he said gravely. Nobody seemed to pay any attention to the fact that he was standing on the table. 'This is to be the goddamndest picture ever made, with a new technique of realism that will even surpass the great Russian school. And the inspiration is that little lady here – ' he motioned to Rose Otto – 'the most modest dinner partner I have ever had in this scurrilous town. Miss Otto, as you know, is the girl who has just broken the record for being buried alive – and at once she was collected by that indefatigable gatherer of celebrities, that magnificent collector of headliners, our lovely hostess, heiress of the great fortune of that late benefactor of mankind, Caleb Smithers, the patent-medicine king.'

Everybody applauded.

'Well,' he said, looking down, 'where was I?'

One of the producers glanced up.

'This was to be the goddamndest picture ever made. I'm all ears.'

'You're telling us,' Heinrich said, laughing, almost falling off the table. Everybody joined in the laughter. In a moment Heinrich went on:

'The goddamdest picture ever made. Yes. Well, the girl in

this picture is buried alive. She has a grasping manager and
he is eager to collect the one-thousand-dollar prize for
breaking the world's record. They have twenty-four hours
to go and it looks like they're in the bag. Well, along comes
a guy who pays his dime to go in and look through the
periscope at this girl buried thirty-feet beneath him. He
speaks to her through the speaking-tube. Now, the point of
this – and we'll emphasize this with camera movement – is
that the girl can't see him. Remember that – she cannot see
him – but she can *hear* him. So they carry on a banal
conversation and the girl who is buried begins to feel that
old sex urge – '

He broke off, looking at Rose Otto.

'No offense, Miss Otto,' he said. 'This isn't you. This is
another girl.'

'Go right ahead,' she said, smiling.

'All right,' Heinrich went on, talking to the chandelier.
'This guy has got sex appeal in his voice. He has got more
sex appeal in his voice than any hundred men in the world.
He is the kind of guy who says hello to a woman and her
pants start smoking. So the girl goes for him. She gets such
a yen for him she asks the manager to dig her up. The
manager thinks she's bug-house – because the manager has
seen this guy. He's the most repulsive-looking man in the
world. His teeth are snags, his nose is eaten away – but the
girl doesn't know this because she has not seen him. She has
only *heard* him. So the manager and the girl have an argu-
ment. He doesn't want to dig her up, because that thousand
bucks is in the bag. And right here the girl plays her trump
card. There is a woman's club in the neighborhood which

has been protesting this very exhibition. The girl threatens
to tell this club that the manager is holding her against her
will – and, boy, that floors him. So he orders the girl dug up
and goes to find the guy who's got that sex in his voice. It'll
take three or four hours to excavate this dame and he's got
plenty of time. He finally locates the little guy in a hamburger
joint. He starts talking to him, telling him what's happened.
The little guy can hardly believe his ears. A woman who
wants him more than she wants any other man? Think what
a close-up that'll make – a close-up that fills the screen – as
it finally dawns on this guy. He's always had to buy his
women before.'

'How're you gonna show that?' the producer said.

'That's the director's problem,' Heinrich said. He continued: 'So the manager, this avaricious bird, gets curious
about what'll happen when the girl gets a look at this little
repulsive guy who's got no nose. He asks him what'll he do
when the girl sees him. But that doesn't worry the little guy.
He says, sure, he knows the girl'll turn and run. That
confuses the manager, whose mind is never above his belt.
Unless they're gonna sleep together, he can't see any point
to the little guy making him dig up his star attraction and
losing that thousand bucks. So he says something like this:
"But if you know she's going to be disappointed when she
sees you, why have me dig her up?" and the little guy looks
up at him and says something like this: "Don't you see? This
girl wants me to the exclusion of all the other men in the
world" – he's been well educated – "and that is the first time
it ever happened. In the two or three hours they are digging
her up, until the actual moment when she sees me, I am the

greatest lover in the world." That puzzles the manager. He doesn't get it. So we start moving the camera in on a big two-shot while he says, "But I don't understand." And the little guy smiles compassionately and replies: "I didn't think you would." Fade-out.'

There was some applause as he got down off the table.

'It stinks,' the producer said.

'All right,' Heinrich said. 'I'll write it as a short story. I'll sell it to an art magazine.'

Mrs. Smithers got up from the table.

'Shall we go into the living-room?' she asked.

They all started out. In the hall I excused myself from Rose Otto and went into the lavatory, through the powder room. Heinrich followed me in and shut the door.

'Like the story?' he asked.

'Sure,' I said, agreeing with him because that is the best way to get along with a drunk.

'I thought it was lousy,' he said. 'You know something?' he said. 'I knew it was going to be lousy before I told it. You know why I told it? You know why I stood on the table? You know why I jump in swimming-pools with my clothes on? You know why I wore a sweatshirt to dinner? All right, I'll tell you. Christ, I know it's wrong. I'll tell you. I know I'm no writer. Why, there are guys walking the boulevard who can write a million times better than I can. I used to be a newspaper reporter. When I came out here, I was still a good reporter, but nobody would give me a job. I starved to death. So I figured that this was a sucker town and that a smart guy could hit big. I started doing screwy things, like I did tonight — and you know what happened? I'll tell you.

The studios fought for me. They thought I was a genius. So now I'm getting two grand a week. You've heard of me, haven't you?'

'Sure,' I said, unlocking the door.

'You're a liar,' he said, missing the bowl, leaking all over the floor. 'I can tell by the way you say that, you're a liar. Are you a stranger in Hollywood?'

'I'm beginning to think so,' I said, going out.

After dinner other people began to drop in and by eleven o'clock the house was full. This was not the same crowd I had seen the night of the first party, the one that Mona had come to. Only two or three who were present then were here now. But it was the same kind of party. Pictures, pictures, pictures, that was all they talked about. I tried to carry on a conversation with the two producers I had met at dinner, hoping to tell them somehow that I would like to have a movie career, but I never had the chance to get that in. Rose Otto and I finally went into the patio, where there was less noise.

The lights were on in the swimming-pool, but nobody was swimming. Several couples were scattered in different parts of the patio talking, but there was no roar of talk out there. Rose Otto and I strolled out by the pool and sat down in deck chairs.

'This is lovely, isn't it?' she asked.

'Yes,' I answered.

She lighted a cigarette.

'Do you know her very well?'

'Mrs. Smithers?'

'Yes.'

'Pretty well. Why?'

'Nothing. I was just wondering why she asked me to this party.'

'Don't you know her?'

'I met her today for the first time. I had lunch with her.'

'How'd you happen to meet her in the first place?'

'Some man came down to the pier and asked me to meet her.'

'Who?'

'I don't know. I'm not much good on names. I'd just come up – that's what we call it when they take you out – and he said she wanted me to be the guest of honor. So I made a date with him and today he brought her down to see me.'

'When was that?'

'This morning.'

That's when I was at the morgue, I thought.

'It's funny her asking me here.'

'Was your name in the newspapers about the new world's record you set?' I asked.

'Yes. Pictures too.'

'That's why,' I said.

'She's nice.'

'Yes, she is. – Are you trying to get into pictures?'

She laughed.

'No.'

'No?' I asked. I was surprised.

'No.'

'You're certainly pretty enough.'

'But I can't act.'

'You don't have to act. There's a lot of girls in pictures who can't act.'

'That's what she said. She told me she would get me a test if I came to the party.'

I got a little sore at Mrs. Smithers. She'd promised to help me too – and she had promised me first.

'So I came.'

'But you said you weren't trying to get into pictures.'

'I'm not. That's not the reason I came. I'll tell you if you won't laugh at me.'

'I won't laugh.'

'I came because I've never been to a party like this before. I knew what it would be like and I've always wanted to see one.'

I felt relieved when she said that. I felt better when I knew she was no rival for Mrs. Smithers's help.

'I think that's a good reason,' I said. 'Has anybody here besides Mrs. Smithers said anything about a test? Any of the producers?'

'No – and it wouldn't matter if they did. I'll stick to my own racket. I'm tops in that and I can make a good living at it. I'd be foolish to throw that away.'

'I guess you would,' I said. 'Want to go swimming?'

'It's too cold. Besides, for the next week I'm not going to do anything but sit. I go to Coney Island next week – in New York – and start all over again.'

'Aw-o-o-o-o-o-o-o-o!' somebody shouted. 'Aw-o-o-o-o-o-o-o-o!'

I looked around. It was Heinrich high up in a eucalyptus tree in the patio. He had on nothing but shorts.

'Aw-o-o-o-o-o-o!' he yelled, hanging by one hand, imitating Weissmuller.

141

Everybody ran out of the living-room to look at him.

Rose Otto smiled.

'He's crazy, isn't he?' she said.

'Yes,' I replied, looking at all the guests staring up at him in amazement. 'He's crazy like a fox.'

...chapter
eight

I was getting a blanket out of the closet when I heard Mona's voice saying: 'Who's there? Who is it?'

'Me,' I said, coming back into the living-room.

She was standing on the landing at the head of the stairs in pajamas. 'You scared me.'

'I tried not to make any noise,' I said.

'I wasn't asleep. I was reading.'

She came downstairs in her bare feet.

'What's the matter?' she asked.

'Nothing.'

I put the blanket on the davenport and moved the pillows.

'Something must be wrong. I thought you'd moved out.'

'I'm moving back in,' I said, taking off my coat. I stopped, looking at her. 'If it's all right with you.'

'Of course it's all right with me. What happened?'

'Nothing.'

She put her hands on her hips. I continued removing my coat and tie.

'Do you think it's wise to fight with her?'

'You didn't use to say that,' I said.

'Things are different now. You can't afford to displease her.'

'I haven't had a fight. Not a word was spoken. She had another party and I didn't like it and I walked out. You don't call that a fight, do you?'

'What'll she think when she finds you gone?'

'I don't care what she thinks,' I said. I sat down, taking off my shoes. 'If she calls on the phone you tell her you haven't seen me.'

She walked over and pulled on the floor lamp and then drew the drapes across the front window. She came back and sat on the davenport.

'You shouldn't have done that,' she said finally. 'Don't you realize that she put up the bail money so you could get out of jail? She can revoke that any time she wants to. If she revokes it you'll have to go back to jail.'

'I didn't stop to think about that,' I said. 'But it doesn't make any difference. I'm going to stay here tonight and if I have to I'll go back tomorrow. Maybe I can get Abie to go my bond.'

'But what about your picture career that she was going to arrange for you?'

'You know as much about it as I do. She could help me if she wanted to. I know that. What she's waiting on, I don't know.'

'Certainly she can help you if she wanted to. Do you think she'll ever want to?'

'What do you mean?'

'Simply this. I don't think she has any intention of helping you. She wants you all to herself.'

I shook my head.

'She asked Arthur Wharton to give me a test, didn't she?'

'And what happened?'

'Well – '

'Go on. What happened?'

'Wharton was going away.'

'How can a guy as big as you be so dumb?' she asked. 'That was a come-on. She did that to impress you. She knew Wharton had no intention of giving you a test. She knew he was going to give you the run-around.'

I had thought the same thing, without putting it into those words. Now I knew the reason I had not put it into those words was that I was afraid of the truth.

'I think you're wrong,' I said, still not wanting to admit it.

'Maybe I am,' she said. She got up. 'Well, this is on your own head. You wouldn't listen to me, so you get out of this the best way you can. Maybe it's better for you to learn things the hard way, at that.'

'I'll get out of it,' I said. 'I'll get that bond money somewhere else. I'll see Abie in the morning.'

'You do that,' she said, going upstairs. 'Get him to buy me a Rolls-Royce too.'

She paused on the landing, looking down.

'Good night.'

'Good night.' . . .

I did not get to sleep right away. I lay there, looking out the window at that raggledy palm tree in the moonlight, thinking. It seemed to me that my life all of a sudden had become terribly involved. Why was all this happening to me? I couldn't remember doing anything to cause it. All I wanted was to succeed in pictures; and now I felt that every minute I was getting farther and farther away from pictures. It didn't seem I was in Hollywood at all. I might just as well have been hopping cars in a drive-in stand, wearing a uniform, for all the good I was doing myself. I felt trapped.

Mona was up bright and early in the morning, around seven o'clock, fixing breakfast.

'Didn't you hear the telephone ringing this morning?' she asked.

'No. When?'

'About three o'clock.'

'I didn't hear it,' I said.

'She certainly was anxious to find you. It rang every five minutes until four thirty.'

'You didn't tell her I was here, did you?'

'I didn't tell her anything. I didn't answer it. – Here, sit down and eat.'

I sat down and picked up a piece of toast and started eating it, but I wasn't hungry.

'She'll come sailing in here any minute. What're you going to tell her?'

'I don't know,' I said.

'Well, you'd better start thinking.'

'I thought about it last night after I got in bed, but I didn't get anywhere. I guess I'd better hurry up and out of here. I don't want to be here when she comes.'

'You think that's the answer?'

'I don't know what the answer is,' I said impatiently. 'I just don't want to be here when she comes.'

'If you're going to have a showdown you may as well have it

and get it over with. You can't put it off forever, you know.'

I took a little coffee.

'I want to see Abie first.'

She laughed.

'You don't seriously think he'll put up that bond money, do you?'

'I can ask him, can't I?'

'Sure. You can ask the first person you meet on Vine Street too.'

She was speaking in the same tone she had used last night. It was beginning to get on my nerves.

'I don't see why you're so sarcastic,' I said. 'You act as if you were glad I got in this mess.'

'I'm not glad at all,' she said. 'And I didn't mean to be sarcastic.'

'Well – maybe it wasn't sarcasm. But you've changed. I don't understand what's happened to everything.'

'I haven't changed and nothing's happened to anything but you. Everything else is just the same. It's you. If you'd had any guts you wouldn't have listened to this bitch in the first place. I told you what she was.'

I got up from the table. I couldn't stand it any longer.

'But don't you see,' I said helplessly, 'I thought she could help me in pictures. My God, you don't seem able to get it through your head that I've *got* to hit. I've been out here seven months and I've done nothing. But everybody in my home town thinks I'm already doing big things. It's just a question of time until they find out I'm still unknown. I can't let that happen.'

'Why can't you?' she asked in a calm voice.

'What?' I said.

'Why can't you?'

I shook my head.

'It's just no use,' I said. 'You just don't get it.'

'I do get it,' she said. 'You wrote a lot of lies to your mother about how well you were doing and she got the newspaper to print them. Home-Town Boy Makes Good. And now you're in a panic because you think unless you *do* hurry up and make good they'll find out you've lied.'

'That's it,' I said.

She laughed.

'You don't think you're the first guy that ever wrote lies back to his home town, do you? Everybody does that. I do it myself. But I don't lie awake nights worrying about whether somebody'll find out they're lies. I don't give a damn.'

'Don't you?'

'Certainly not. Well,' she said, pushing her chair back, 'I've got an eight-o'clock call. You want to drive me over and keep the car?'

'No,' I said. 'I think I'll stick around here.'

'I thought you didn't want to see Smithers.'

'If I'm going to have a showdown I may as well have it and get it over with,' I said. 'I can't put it off forever.'

She smiled the kind of smile you smile just before you go into a pleased laugh, and I suddenly knew why she was smiling. Those words I had said weren't mine but hers. I smiled too.

'That's more like it,' she said, going into the living-room, putting on her hat. 'Did you see where the strike was over?'

148

'No,' I said.

'You didn't? It's in the headlines. Didn't you see the paper?'

'No. Where is it?'

'On the kitchen table. You sat here looking at it for five minutes.'

'I had other things on my mind.'

She seemed very happy now.

'Yes, sir. They won it without even walking out. The producers have got more sense than I thought they had. We've got a united front now. There won't be any more squawking about overtime and there won't be any more working all hours of the night without some kind of adjustment. Imagine Crawford and Cagney and people like that going to bat for us. Doesn't it make you feel good to think about it?'

'I suppose so,' I said.

She patted me on the shoulder.

'You'll be all right when you get this other thing off your mind. Now, remember – don't budge an inch unless you're convinced she will not revoke the bond. I wish I could be here to help you.'

'You seem pretty sure she's coming. What if she doesn't come? What if she just calls up the judge and tells him she withdraws from the bond?'

'She won't do that. She'll come.' She stopped at the door. 'Ralph – if I were you I wouldn't say anything to Abie about that bond business. He'd think you were a fool.'

'He'd be thinking right,' I said.

'Well, I hope you're still here when I get back.'

'I'll be here,' I said.

...*chapter nine*

MOVIE STARS WIN STRIKE FIGHT, the headline said, and I read the story. When I had finished reading it I didn't know much more than I did when I had started. The whole thing was just a blur of print to me. I was worried about Mrs. Smithers and what she would do when I told her I never wanted to see her again. This was what I tried to tell her yesterday in a nice way in the patio, but she never let me finish.

'Mona's right,' I told myself. 'I never should have got mixed up with her in the first place.'

The telephone rang and I jumped a foot. When I picked up the receiver I was shaking all over.

But it wasn't Mrs. Smithers. It was somebody in the coroner's office.

'Is Mona Matthews there?'

'No, sir.'

'This where she lives?'

'Yes, sir. She's at work.'

'Who is this?'

'Ralph Carston.'

'You know anything about a girl named Dorothy Trotter?'

'Yes, sir, I know her.'

'We're trying to find out where she lives and who her relatives are.'

'She lives in Ohio somewhere. I don't know the name of the town.'

'Where can we get in touch with Miss Matthews?'

'At Excelsior studio. But I'm sure she doesn't know either. I think I remember hearing Dorothy say once she didn't have any relatives.'

'Are you pretty sure of that?'

'Pretty sure, yes, sir. But Mona would know. You leave your number and I'll have her call you.'

'Mutual 9211. Coroner's office. If we can't locate any relatives for this girl we'll have to cremate the body ourselves. Tell her to call right away.'

'Yes, sir.'

I hung up and called Excelsior, finally getting connected with the soundstage where the Eubanks company was working. The man who answered the phone said Mona wasn't there, that he didn't know where she was, that Miss Eubanks wasn't on the set yet. I gave him my name, begging him to have Mona get in touch with me right away, telling him it was a matter of life or death. He said he'd do that little thing.

Dorothy, I thought, Dorothy – a faint pain hit me in the heart and I breathed three or four times in rapid succession before I exhaled once. This is what I should have felt yesterday when I saw her body, I thought. . . .

I finally got up and went into the kitchen and started washing the breakfast dishes because there was nothing else to do.

151

About ten minutes later Mona came in. Her face was pale.

'You didn't have to come home,' I said. 'I only told the man who took the message that it was life or death so you would call me.'

'What?' she said.

'Didn't you get the message?'

'What message?'

'I called you ten or fifteen minutes ago.'

'Called me?'

'Yes. The coroner called about Dorothy. He wanted to know about her relatives – what to do with her body.'

'She hasn't got any relatives. She's an orphan. That's what she always said.'

'You'd better call the coroner. The number's written down there.'

She went over to the desk and dialled the number, asking for the coroner's office. She told them who she was and asked what it was they wanted to know about Dorothy Trotter. 'Yes, sir. From Ohio somewhere, I can't tell you. . . . No, sir, I'm sure she didn't. She always said she was an orphan. . . . No, sir, I don't. The only one would be some man back there she was once engaged to marry, but all I know is he works in a radio shop. . . . Yes, sir, I know it isn't much help, but that's all I ever heard her say. . . . Yes, sir, I suppose that's best. How much will it cost?. . . . The county will. . . . Yes, sir. Good-bye.'

She put the receiver on the hook, turning around.

'Good God!' she said. 'Cremation – '

'I know how you feel,' I said.

'Good God!' she said, getting up, going slowly upstairs. . . .

I don't know how long I stood there. I knew how Mona felt and I didn't want to interfere. I didn't know what she was doing up there in the bedroom, I could hear no sound; probably crying. If so, that was good. It would make her feel better.

After a while I went up to see what she was doing. She was sitting on the side of the bed smoking a cigarette. She had not been crying.

'Mona,' I said, 'hadn't you better get back to the studio?'

'I'm not working there any more,' she said. She stood up straightening her dress. 'I got fired.'

'Fired? For what?'

'I was six minutes late on the set.'

She started out.

'But,' I said, following her downstairs, 'they certainly wouldn't fire you for being six minutes late.'

'No? Well, they did.'

'What a tough bunch that Excelsior outfit must be!'

She put out her cigarette in the ash-tray on the desk.

'They're all tough – and they're all bastards,' she said. 'You'll find that out one of these days.'

One of these days. . . .

'But it seems so silly,' I said. 'Didn't you have an excuse?'

'No excuse in the world would have done me any good,' she said grimly. 'They were out to get me and they did. Johnny Hill said they would. It's strange, isn't it?' she said, looking at me, trying to smile, 'that nobody pays any attention to what anybody else says. Believe me, after this I'll never get sore at you.'

'It's probably a good thing,' I said. 'A stand-in never gets any place. It's all for the best.'

She smiled.

'Everything happens for the best. What happened to Dorothy was for the best and what's happened to me is for the best. What'll happen to you is for the best. Did you hear from the bitch yet?'

'No,' I said. 'You don't suppose she's called the judge and told him to cancel the bond?'

'When she does that, you'll know it. There'll be a cop right in your lap when that happens.'

'That's a cheerful thing to say.'

'It's been a cheerful day.' She walked towards the door. 'Want a coke?'

'No.'

'What's this, suh?' she said, imitating me. 'You-all from th' ol' South and don't want no cokey-coley?'

'That's not very funny,' I said.

'I-all is sho' s'prised at you-all, suh. Well, suh, I-all will be back t'reckly.'

She stopped at the door, turning around.

'Nuts,' she said.

I sat around for the next thirty minutes, waiting for Mona to come back, waiting for the phone to ring – or expecting any minute to have Mrs. Smithers walk in the front door. Two or three times I started to call her, but I couldn't get up my nerve.

Johnny Hill suddenly came barging in like a maniac.

'Where is she?' he asked. 'Where is she?'

'She went to the drug store,' I said. 'What's the matter with you?'

'When's she coming back?'

'She should have been back before now. What's the matter?'

'I just quit my job.'

He started walking up and down the floor.

'Again?' I asked.

'This time for good,' he said. 'I'm through with these goddam cheap moving-picture factories. You hear what they did to Mona?'

'They fired her. How'd you know?'

'How'd I know?' He broke off.

Mona came in.

'I told you, didn't I?' he said, shaking his head in her face. 'Goddam it, I told you what'd happen.'

'Sit down and get the weight off your feet and stop yelling and waving your arms,' she said.

Johnny cooled down a little.

'I gather you've heard the news,' Mona said.

'I hear everything. I went down to the set about an hour ago looking for you. When I saw Eubanks had another stand-in I asked her what'd happened to you. She told me. She said you were late again and generally unreliable and that she was compelled to let you go, simply compelled.'

'That's right,' Mona said.

'That's the phoniest excuse I ever heard. I asked her why she didn't tell you the real reason. She pretended to be very astounded, and then I told her that I know the front office had dropped a hint in her ear and that she was looking for any legitimate reason to give you the can. Well, we had words and we got louder and louder and finally the director horned in and there were some more words and he ordered me off the set and then there were some words and finally I took a sock at him – you know how I am when I get excited.'

'Like you are now,' Mona said.

He calmed down and lowered his voice.

'There was a hell of a row when I got back to the office – it seems the director had phoned the production office, and the production office had phoned publicity – and so there were still some more words, only these were nice and juicy, and I walked out and told them to take my check and stick it.'

'Oh, Johnny,' Mona said, 'you shouldn't have done that.'

'I was getting sick of that joint anyway. Now, look, we're going to carry this thing to the Guild. We'll take it into court. By God, we'll take it to the Supreme Court. They're not going to get away with this.'

'I'd rather forget it,' Mona said.

'You can't forget it. Goddam it, you've got to make a test case out of this. What the hell's the Guild for? Just such travesties as this. Jesus, if I ever heard of a grievance, it's this.'

'I agree with you,' Mona said. 'I'm sore myself and I thought about going to the Guild too. But what would happen? Eubanks would cover the studio. She'd swear I was unreliable. She'd say she fired me for being late two mornings in a row – and she'd be right because I was late. Morally, they're guilty, but legally they're in the clear.'

Johnny thought that over. He sat down and lighted a cigarette.

'I never thought of that. I should have known they'd be clever enough to make this thing airtight.'

'I thought you were smarter than this, Johnny.'

'Smarter than what?'

'To get in an uproar about something like this. The last time you were here you warned me about this very thing and told me to lay off. Yet you've done almost the same thing you told me not to.'

That's exactly what I was thinking too.

Johnny got up and stood glowering.

'It's not the same at all,' he said. 'Anyway, what difference does it make? I'm the way I am and I can't help it. I act on impulse. Goddam it, if I didn't, do you think I'd just be a forty-dollar-a-week publicity man? If I could control my temper and my emotions I'd be a big executive. I can't help it, can I?'

He started pacing the floor again.

'Don't get conceited,' he said. 'I didn't do this because of you – not solely because of you. You just happened to be a friend of mine, that's all. I'd have been just as sore if it'd been somebody I didn't even know. You're just a symbol. . . . Maybe you should have let Eubanks make you.'

'God knows she tried hard enough,' Mona said. 'But when I go in for that sort of thing I'm certainly not going into open competition with a colored maid.'

157

'The goddam Lesbian,' Johnny said. 'I'd like to write what I know about her.'

'Why don't you? You could sell it to one of the fan magazines. You know how they go for the home life of the stars.'

'You mark my words,' Johnny said, pointing with his cigarette. 'I'll show up these studios someday. I'll make a picture of my own – and I'll show it if I have to pack it around the country on my back. That or I'll write a novel about them.'

He walked a little more, puffing on his cigarette. Mona and I looked at each other, saying nothing.

'Any liquor in the house?' Johnny asked.

'No.'

'Mind if I bring a bottle?'

'Of course not.'

'Be right back,' he said, going out the door.

I looked at Mona.

'You don't want him getting drunk here, do you?'

'Why not? He'll get drunk somewhere. Don't you like him?'

'He's all right.'

'He's better than that,' she said. 'At least he's got guts enough to hate something.'

'But suppose Mrs. Smithers comes? We can't talk very well if he's drinking.'

'I do hope she won't be too shocked,' Mona said.

...*chapter ten*

Mrs. Smithers arrived about an hour later. I was glad because I wanted to get it over with, and I was glad too that Johnny was not drunk. I had never seen him drunk, but I knew what he was capable of and I didn't want him involving the situation for me. He was in a beautiful glow. Mona was still nursing her first drink, while I had had none. I looked anxiously at Mrs. Smithers's face the first few minutes she was in the room, before she took off her things, trying to see if there were any danger signals. She appeared as if nothing out of the ordinary had happened, and my spirits rose.

'Are you *the* Mrs. Smithers?' Johnny asked.

'Is there another one?' she said, smiling, her eyes very innocent.

That remark made me feel even better. 'I hope she stays that way,' I thought. 'It'll make it easier for me to say what I've got to say.'

'I'm delighted to meet you at last, Mrs. Smithers,' Johnny said. 'I've been wanting to do a story about you for a long time.'

Mrs. Smithers fluttered her eyebrows.

'Johnny's a writer,' Mona said.

'Yes,' he went on, 'for a long time I've wanted to do a

serious story about you. For a big magazine like the *Saturday Evening Post* or *Collier's* – or even one of the better fan magazines. Hollywood's Unofficial Hostess. How you entertain all the celebrities and everything.'

Mrs. Smithers beamed.

'Well,' she said, 'you seem to know all about me.'

'You're a famous woman, my dear Mrs. Smithers,' Johnny said seriously. 'Do you know that you've replaced Pickford and Fairbanks as the Number One hostess of this glamorous village?'

I tried to signal Mona to make Johnny stop. He was laying it on pretty thick and I was afraid she would finally realize he was kidding her. I couldn't catch Mona's eye. She wouldn't look at me.

'Hadn't we better go to lunch?' I asked Mrs. Smithers.

'Listen to him,' Johnny said. 'Trying to take the guest of honor away. Why, you've just got here, Mrs. Smithers, why do you put up with a child like that? What possible interest could that naive, unspoiled youth have for you?' He looked at me. 'You speak when you're spoken to. Lunch indeed!'

'Not yet,' she said to me. 'Later.'

'Much later,' Johnny said. 'Fair lady, you'll drink with me, won't you?'

'Of course I will.'

'Of course you will. Let's get a drink while I explain what happened to Ralph last night – why he did not stay at the party. It was all my fault. I wanted a story – the story of his life.'

They went into the kitchen, arm in arm. I turned to Mona.

'You told him about last night,' I said. 'Why? What else did you tell him?'

She looked at me, and when she spoke, her voice was steady.

'I told him the whole story – all of it.'

'But why?'

'You want to get away, don't you? You don't want her to revoke that bond, do you?'

'No.'

'Then just keep your shirt on.'

Johnny and Mrs. Smithers came back out of the kitchen, laughing and talking.

'I was just telling Ethel – ' he turned to her, smiling – 'you don't mind if I call you Ethel?'

She shook her head.

'Good. You can call me Johnny. – I was just telling Ethel how marvellous she is to sit here with us, in this modest little bungalow, drinking and conversing, when she could be in any one of fifty other places, mansions, with distinguished people.'

'I like everybody, Johnny,' she said. She took a couple of swallows of the drink. 'Would you really write the story of my life?'

Johnny sat down by her.

'Would I? Ethel, now that I've met you I'd write it for nothing. I wouldn't take a cent. It would be that much of a pleasure.'

He put his hand on her leg, casually. I could see her eyes open a little, but otherwise she paid no attention. Mona nudged me and I nodded to tell her that I saw it.

'Drink up,' Johnny said. 'You're way behind.'

Mrs. Smithers looked at us.

'Aren't you two drinking?'

'I'm not,' I said.

Mona held up her glass.

'Don't wait for me.'

'A couple of softies,' Johnny said. 'Gimme your glass, Ethel.'

He took it and went into the kitchen.

When I told Abie I wanted two bottles of Bourbon and six bottles of ginger ale his mouth opened in astonishment.

'For you?' he asked.

'Of course not,' I said. 'Some people dropped in. I don't drink.'

He looked at me thoughtfully.

'I'll pay for them,' I said. 'And I haven't forgotten that twenty I owe you. I'll pay that too.'

'I got faith in you, Ralph,' he said, getting the liquor from the glass case beside him. 'Only don't bust my faith.'

'I won't, Abie,' I said.

I paid him and started back. As I passed the office Mrs. Anstruther stopped me and handed me the mail. There were three or four letters, all for Mona.

I gave Johnny the liquor and he joined Mrs. Smithers in the kitchen. When I handed Mona the letters she looked at them and then glanced at me quickly, coloring a little, putting them in the pocket of her coat.

In a minute Johnny and Mrs. Smithers came out of the kitchen with fresh drinks. They were completely absorbed

in each other. They acted as if there was nobody else in the
world.

They sat down on the davenport, close together. Johnny
was drunk, but not too drunk to know what he was doing. I
saw him look at Mona over Mrs. Smithers's shoulder and
wink. He cupped his hand under her breast and she moved
it away.

'You know something, Ethel?' he said. 'This morning
when I got up and stood in front of the mirror without any
clothes on and I took a look at my superb equipment, I said
to myself: "Hill, you ought to have a bright future – and
look at you – a bum."'

'You're not a bum, Johnny,' she said in a thickish voice.
'I won't have you being a bum. You can't be my director if
you're going to be a bum.'

'All right. I'm not a bum. We're gonna give Mona and
Ralph the leads in this picture.'

'No. I love Mona and Ralph, but they can't be in it. Got
to have names.'

'Now, Ethel, you talk like a goddam producer.'

'Got to have names. Box office.'

'I'm the director. I'll pick the cast.'

'I'm the producer. I'm putting up the money.'

You've certainly covered a lot of ground, I thought.

Johnny looked at me.

'Commercial, she is. Mercenary.'

He turned back to her, putting his hand under her dress.
She shoved it away.

'Not here,' she said in a voice that was meant to be a
whisper. 'Not here.'

163

'Well, for Christ's sake, let's go where we can,' Johnny said, not caring who heard him. 'Let's go over to my place.'

'No, we'll go to my place.'

'All right, we'll go to your place.'

She made an effort to get up.

'Mona and Ralph'll come too.'

'They don't want to go.'

She stopped trying to get up and stared at him.

'They'll go or we'll stay here.'

I looked at Mona. She shrugged.

'All right,' I said, not because I wanted to go to her house but because I wanted to get them out of the bungalow.

We finally got their things together, and when we went out, Mona had hold of Johnny and I had hold of Mrs. Smithers, walking out of the court to her car, trying to be nonchalant, feeling that everybody was staring at us from behind the curtains.

...*chapter eleven*

It was after five o'clock. Johnny and Mrs. Smithers were off in another part of the house, upstairs somewhere, and Mona and I were sitting in the patio.

'How much longer are we going to stay here?' I asked.

'I don't know.'

'I don't see much point to this,' I said.

'Well, apparently they're having a good time. We haven't seen them for an hour and a half.'

'If we wait for them we'll be sitting here all night,' I said. 'They've forgotten we're here. They're drunk. They're probably asleep.'

'No, they aren't asleep. I hear an occasional suspicious noise from up above. They'll be down in a minute.'

'It's a long minute. That's what you said an hour ago.'

'Why are you so jittery? You're not jealous are you?'

'Of course not. You know better than that.'

'Well, calm yourself. What would you be doing if you weren't here?'

'I don't know,' I replied. 'I want to go down to Central Casting.'

'For what?'

'To have a talk with them. I don't understand why you and I can't get work.'

'You're a little late thinking about that.'

'I've had other things to think of until now. I'm getting a little desperate.'

She did not say anything for a moment.

'It wouldn't do any good to see Central. There simply isn't enough work to go around. I'm desperate too. But we aren't by ourselves.'

I looked at the pool, thinking this was no consolation to me, that it didn't improve my morale to think about other people being desperate. I made up my mind then and there that tomorrow I would go to Excelsior and see Mr. Balter if I had to drive through the wall with a truck. Yes, and I was going to see all the other studios too. I was going to go to every casting office in town. I was through being put off.

'Of course,' Mona was saying, 'you're not in as bad a spot as I am. Every studio in town has probably got me on the blacklist by now.' She was very thoughtful. 'I'll have a hell of a time getting a job after what happened with Eubanks.'

'I don't see why, since you won the strike. Johnny said he'd take it to the Guild for you. What's the use of having a Guild if you don't use it?'

'I explained that to you this morning. It wouldn't do any good. You know what I think? I think your whole future is mapped out from the day you're born, from the day you're even conceived, and that no matter what you do, you can't beat it. There's no escape.'

'You mean girls like Crawford and Colbert and Dietrich

and the others were born to be movie stars? I don't. It just happened.'

She smiled.

'Maybe I didn't say it right,' she said. 'I'm thinking it right, though. The way I'm thinking it is right. Skip it.'

Johnny opened the door upstairs that led down the steps to the patio and yelled: 'How's the weather down there?'

'All right,' Mona said. 'How's it up where you are?'

'Equatorial – equatorial,' he said.

He did not appear to be drunk now. He had his coat and tie off and his sleeves were rolled up.

'Johnny,' Mona said, 'how long before you're coming down?'

'Hours,' he replied. 'Days. Maybe weeks.'

'Look, Johnny – Ralph and I are getting a little bored down here alone. Do you think you'd mind if we went home?'

'Not at all,' he said. 'Just a minute while I check with the maitre d' – '

He stepped back inside and a moment later Mrs. Smithers appeared. She was wearing a négligé and was trying to be very dignified.

'You're not going?' she said.

You old poop, I thought.

'If you don't mind, Mrs. Smithers – ' Mona said politely. She looked at me and I knew she was thinking the same thing I was. 'We've got to get back to the telephone. This is about the time the work calls starts coming through – '

'They're slaves,' Johnny said to her. 'They're slaves to the telephone.'

167

'Certainly, children,' she said. 'Certainly. But you are perfectly welcome to come back later.'

'Thank you. Good-bye.'

'Good-bye,' she said, smiling sweetly, as Johnny took her by the arm, easing her inside.

Mona and I stood up. Johnny stepped out on the balcony, leaning over.

'It's okay,' he said in a loud whisper. 'It's okay about him.' He pointed to me. 'See you tomorrow.' He waved his hand and went inside.

I looked around the patio, thinking how wonderful all this had seemed to me once, thinking about the first dinner I had had here, with the butlers and everything, when I took my first lesson in how to eat, not quite so sure now that I would ever have a place like this, not quite so sure. . . .

'Come on,' I heard Mona say.

'I'm coming,' I said.

...*chapter twelve*

That night I discovered the park at De Longpre and Chero-
kee. I was walking around the streets in the neighborhood,
Fountain and Livingston and Cahuenga, because they were
dark and lonely, looking at all the small houses, telling
myself that these were where Swanson and Pickford and
Chaplin and Arbuckle and the others used to live in the good
old days, when making movies was fun and not business,
walking around thinking of those old days and what a shame
it was they had to pass, feeling a personal loss that was still
very warm and nostalgic, like a visit to a graveyard where
your grandfather and grandmother and all your relatives
are buried. You don't feel that you are a stranger even
though you have never visited the graveyard before because
the tombstones represent something and somebody you have
known a long, long time, and loved, and it was like that now.
I was no stranger on these streets. . . .

I came upon the park suddenly. At first I thought it was
the yard of some house, because you don't expect a city
park to be as small as this one was; it covered only half a
block. But when I saw the benches around and the sign
telling you to keep off the grass, I knew what it was. I sat
down on a wet bench and looked around. There was nobody

else there, which was right and proper. It was still misting a little, and all the other fools were inside their little houses.

There was a red haze above the boulevard eight blocks north, thrown up by the neon signs. The only building you could see over the tops of the small houses across the street was the Catholic church on Sunset, its white spire sticking straight up into the black sky.

Presently I was aware that there was someone else in the park. I looked around, behind me, and saw a figure silhouetted in the light from the single globe that was fixed on top of some kind of grass shelter. I couldn't tell whether it was a man or a woman. It was on its knees in front of a small fountain, in an attitude of prayer, its hands moving rapidly in some kind of Oriental gesture. This continued for a few minutes and then the figure got up and walked past me out of the park. It was a woman, a middle-aged woman, dressed entirely in black.

I walked over to the fountain. It was a fish-pond and what I had thought was a fountain was a statue. The statue was about three feet high, a figure with arms at its side, its head lifted. I leaned forward, looking at the tablet.

ASPIRATION
Erected in memory of Rudolph
Valentino

1895   1926

Presented by his friends and admirers from every walk of life – in all parts of the world – in appreciation of the Happiness brought to them by his cinema portrayals.

On the railing around the pond, in front of the statue, was the single gardenia the woman had left.

'I know how you feel, lady,' I said to her in my mind. 'I know exactly how you feel. . . .'

When I got back to the bungalow, Mona was still up, writing a letter. On the desk was a copy of the Oklahoma City *Daily News*. That was a bad sign. When she felt blue she always got her home-town newspaper and read it from cover to cover. She looked at me as I came in, but did not say anything until she had addressed the envelope. Then she asked where I'd been.

'Walking around,' I said.

She put a lot of two-cent stamps on the envelope and stood up.

'I'll be back in a minute,' she said, reaching for her coat.

'You can mail that tomorrow,' I said. 'It won't be collected until morning anyway.'

'That's not the reason I'm mailing it,' she said. 'I want to get it over with before I lose my nerve.'

She went out. . . .

That was the letter that did it. That was the letter. I know it was.

I did not sleep much that night. I lay awake thinking of what I was going to say to Mr. Balter and all the casting directors I was going to see in the morning. With Mrs. Smithers out of my life I knew it was up to me. I could hardly wait to get going. I would say to them . . .

171

...*chapter thirteen*

It was a little after ten o'clock that I called Excelsior and asked the operator the name of the publicity director. She said Egan and asked me if I wanted to be connected. I said yes.

'Is Mr. Egan there?' I asked when the other girl answered.

'Who's calling?'

'Carston of the Los Angeles *Times*.'

'Just a moment,' she said. Then: 'Go ahead – here's Mr. Egan.'

'Hello.'

'Mr. Egan?'

'Yes.'

'Carston of the *Times*,' I said, trying to be very professional. 'I'm in the neighborhood and I'd like to see you a moment. It's about Johnny Hill – '

'Hill doesn't work here any more.'

'I know that. But I've got some information you ought to have.'

'Why – okay.'

'Leave a pass for me, will you? Ralph Carston.'

'Okay.'

I hurried over to the studio, hoping he would not be

curious enough to phone the *Times*, hoping the cop at the information desk was not the one who knew me. If it was, I was going to bluff it through anyway. But it wasn't. The pass was there. I took it and went inside, walking to the end of the corridor before I stopped a girl and asked her where Mr. Balter's office was. She said it was upstairs.

I went upstairs and went into his office. A girl was sitting in a corner at a desk beside a door marked: PRIVATE.

'Is Mr. Balter in?'

'I'm expecting him any minute,' she said. 'Can I help you?'

'No – I'm just on the lot. I'll wait.'

I sat down and picked up a copy of the two daily trade papers, looking at them, but not seeing what they said. I was rehearsing my speech. . . .

In about five minutes the door opened and in walked Mr. Balter.

'Hello, there, Mr. Balter,' I said, going to him with my hand outstretched, very nervous.

'Hello,' he said, not too cordially, shaking hands. He didn't know who I was and I saw him glance questioningly at the secretary.

'Remember me? I'm Ralph Carston.'

'Oh, yes,' he said, still without enthusiasm. 'How are you?'

'Fine,' I said. 'Fine. Just happened to be on the lot and thought I'd drop in. Can I talk to you a minute?'

'Why – er – I suppose so. Come on into the office.' As he passed the secretary he said: 'Get that boy and girl from Ott's office and tell them to come on over for the test. I won't be a minute.'

173

We went into the office and he closed the door.

'What's on your mind, Carston?' he asked. He did not sit down. He stood almost beside me. 'Sorry I haven't been able to see you before. I've been terribly busy.'

I had in my mind to be hard-boiled and, if necessary, beat the hell out of him, but then I decided in a hurry I'd better be nice because, after all, he might do something for me.

'Well, Mr. Balter,' I said, 'I know that test I made sometime ago wasn't much good. But I've learned a lot since then, and I felt if I came to see you, you would give me another test and maybe a stock contract. I've learned a lot since the last time I saw you.'

'I don't doubt it.'

'I'd be willing to work for almost nothing if I could get a contract. Even twenty-five a week would be all right.'

'I'm sorry, Carston. I can't do anything. That accent – '

'But, Mr. Balter,' I said, 'I had that accent when you brought me out here. It didn't make any difference then.'

He shook his head.

'I brought you out because I thought you would do for a part in a Southern picture we made. I didn't bring you out because we thought you'd be of permanent value.'

'You mean – you mean you didn't think I was going to be a star?'

'Of course not. Our contract was to furnish you transportation both ways – which we did. Simply because you chose to stay here is no fault of ours.'

'But, Mr. Balter,' I said, 'I can act. I'm a good actor. You saw me act. You know I can act – '

'Yes, you were good — on the Little Theater stage. But I'm sorry to say your motion-picture test was a big disappointment.'

'But I've learned since then. I can act now.'

He shook his head again.

'The best thing for you to do is go home,' he said. 'As long as you stay here you'll be unhappy and miserable. Your accent kills you for pictures.'

'I can't help it if I was born in the South,' I said.

'Neither can we. By all means go home, boy. You aren't well.'

My head was swimming. I took hold of the door-knob to brace myself.

'I can't go home,' I heard myself say. 'I can't go home. They think I'm already — no, I can't go home.'

'I'm sorry,' he said. 'I thought when you got the railroad fare you'd go back to Georgia.'

'I was waiting to hear about the test,' I said.

'That check we sent you meant the test was a failure. That's what the check meant.'

My head stopped swimming a little.

'Thanks, Mr. Balter,' I said, turning the knob.

'Wait a minute, Carston. I'm certain I can get the studio to give you another transportation check.'

'Thanks just the same,' I said, going out.

I walked around for an hour. I was empty, but I wasn't hungry. I knew if I had a sandwich or anything it would make me sick, so I drank a malted milk and went home.

Johnny was there with Mona.

175

'Hiya, there, Gawguh,' he said, coming to me with his arm out. 'Boy, do I owe you a debt?'

He hugged me and kissed me on each cheek.

'Imagine,' Mona said. 'Johnny's struck gold.'

'Baby,' Johnny said, 'this is a bonanza. This makes the Comstock lode look like a storm drain. This is what I've been waiting for all my life.'

'He's moved right in,' Mona said.

'Has he?' I said.

'Yes, sir,' he said. 'A nymphomaniac with a million dollars. Jesus, with ten million. Boy, am I going to show this goddam town something now? I'll throw parties that'll dazzle the whole world. Gold plates and gold spoons and diamond-studded chastity belts for all the female guests. In three months I'll be running the most talked-of domicile in the last hundred years. I'll make San Simeon look like a one-room tourist camp. I'll be Lucullus and Ward McAllister rolled into one.'

'Don't forget about the picture you're going to make,' Mona said.

'That can wait.'

'And the book too,' I said. 'Don't forget the novel you're going to write about the extras.'

'That can wait,' he said. 'I'm going to be too busy spending money. And incidentally, Ralph, don't worry about that bond. Ethel won't renege on it. And I'll see that nothing happens at the trial, either. I've got enough dough now to buy the whole Civic Center.'

'Thanks,' I said, but at that moment the trial didn't mean anything to me.

'Well, Johnny,' Mona said, 'I'm happy that you're happy.'
Johnny shook his head.

'It's not happiness – it's excitement. I'm excited because finally I've got the weapons to get back at a lot of bastards I despise. The only thing that counts in this town is dough. And now I've got it, so to all those I don't like I'm turning the other cheek – a golden cheek. I'll fix 'em.' He turned to me. 'No hard feelings, Ralph?'

'Don't be silly,' I said. 'Of course not.'

'That's good. You never were her type. You're much too nice. To know what to do in a situation like this you have to be a son of a bitch. I'm a son of a bitch and that's why it's made to order for me.'

'Oh, I wouldn't say that,' I said.

'Certainly, I'll say it. But people'll come to my parties because practically everybody else in town is a son of a bitch too. The only difference between me and them is I'm out in the open.'

'You should worry,' Mona said.

'The hell with 'em,' he said. 'One thing I've learned in Hollywood is that it's a game you can't play according to the rules. A kick in the scrotum is their idea of fair play. Well, I've got to go out to Jack Schafer's and buy some appropriate clothes. You two need any money?'

'No,' I said. 'Thanks.'

He turned to go.

'I'll have you out to the house one of these nights,' he said.

'You do that,' Mona said.

'I will. So long.'

He went out laughing.

'He acts as if it were a joke,' I said.

'It is a joke,' Mona said. 'It's one of the best jokes I've ever heard.'

I spent the next three days looking for a job. I had decided that I could postpone my movie career for a while, until I could save a little money to take lessons in diction and get rid of my accent. If I was going to do anything in pictures I had to get rid of that accent. I hadn't thought much about it before, but since that talk with Mr. Balter I had thought of nothing else. There was no hurry about me getting into pictures anyway, except for that reason that was always in the back of my mind – that one about the people in my home town. But pictures were going to last a long time. 'Take it easy,' I told myself. 'Get a job and save some money and then go to a good voice teacher and get him to work on that accent.' But jobs were scarce. In the three days I pounded the pavements I found out what everybody meant by unemployment. This was something else I had never paid much attention to before. I did work half a day for Abie at the market, straightening up the canned goods on the shelves and carrying purchases out to the cars of the customers. He paid me a dollar and a half, but he was so swell I told him to apply it on the money he had loaned me that night Dorothy showed up. A dollar and a half. This was very funny to me, getting a dollar and a half while Robert Taylor and Gable and those people made thousands. If they can do it, so can I, I thought. . . .

I saw Mona only nights and I had very little to say to her. She acted strangely, but I thought it was because she was worried too. In four days the rent would be due.

...part
three

...*chapter one*

A couple of days later a letter came from Mother. It was just a regular letter, but with this postscript:

'Butch Siegfried, or George, I should say, married Claire Lyons yesterday and they are coming to Hollywood on their honeymoon. I have given them your address and they are going to look you up. They are both movie fans and so you will know what to do with them. I want you to take time off and be nice to them. I know you are very busy at the studios, but remember the Siegfrieds still own the store and we still owe them money. Ha-ha. Love, Mother.'

I folded the letter, and a clipping fell out. It was about their marriage.

Claire Lyons, I thought. My old sweetheart. If I had stayed home, maybe I would be the one.

I looked up and there was a man standing in the door. He was about thirty-five and heavy-set and was staring at me.

'Is Miss Matthews here?' he asked.

I got up and went to the door.

'She's not here now,' I said.

'Mind if I come in and wait?'

'No – come in.'

I stepped back so he could get in.

'Sit down,' I said.

He sat down on the edge of the davenport, holding his hat in his hand, spinning it on his forefinger.

'You a friend of hers?' he asked.

'Yes.'

'My name's Nate Bagby,' he said. He got up awkwardly, sticking out his hand.

'Mine's Carston,' I said, shaking hands.

Then neither of us said anything for a moment.

'I feel kind of hacked,' he said. 'I ain't never seen Miss Matthews.'

'Haven't you?'

He shook his head, reaching into his pocket. He took out a snapshot and handed it to me.

'That her?'

'Yes.'

He seemed pleased.

'How long've you known her?'

'A long, long time,' I said.

'Is she as pretty as this picture?'

'She's beautiful,' I said.

'That's swell.'

'How long have you known her?'

'We been writing to each other 'bout three weeks, but I ain't never seen her. We only swapped pictures. She liked mine and I liked hers. Hollywood's some place, ain't it?'

'Yes,' I said. 'Where do you live?'

'Up in the San Joaquin valley. I got a few fruit trees up there. First time I ever been down to Hollywood.'

'It's quite a place, all right,' I said.

'Never had no reason to come before. I guess coming to get a wife is enough reason though, wouldn't you say so?'

'Yes – that's plenty of reason. How'd you and Mona happen to start writing to each other?'

'I had an ad in *Lonesome Hearts* magazine. Not many girls up in my neck of the country. Least not with class – she's classy, ain't she?'

'Yes – she's classy. When is this marriage coming off?'

'Right away. Got my car outside all filled with gas and oil. We're going to Las Vegas. Got a three-day law in California, you know.'

'Yes, I know.'

Suddenly there was Mona. She and the man looked at each other, not speaking. She knew who he was.

'Excuse me,' I said, getting up before either could say anything to stop me. I went through the kitchen, out the back way to the street.

The sun was shining, the kind of sun I'd always been afraid of before when I felt like this because of what it would show me, but now I didn't care. I walked along, wondering what I was going to do, thinking about Butch Siegfried, who was coming out on his honeymoon to visit his boyhood playmate who was a successful picture player, thinking about another successful picture player named Dorothy Trotter, thinking home, home, home, about the fellows I grew up with who were now married and had kids and regular jobs and regular salaries, who were doing the same old thing in the same old way and would go on doing it forever, the same thoughts I had had a million times before, only now, for the first time, I realized that maybe they had the right idea. *There's no escape*, Mona had said, and she was proving it by going back to something she had desperately tried to run away from; and then I said something to myself I had never said before (but which I now knew had always been in the back of my mind): *I should have stayed home*. . . .

I turned off Vine Street onto Hollywood Boulevard, going west, telling myself I was crazy to admit that even now it was too late. I hadn't stayed home, I was here, on the famous boulevard, in Hollywood, where miracles happen, and maybe today, maybe the next minute some director would pick me out passing by. . . .